Grave Wind

The Haunting Dahlia Series

Book One

Janice Tremayne

Copyright © 2025 Janice Tremayne
www.janicetremayne.com
author@janicetremayne.com
First published in Australia in 2025

Cover illustration and design by Momir Borocki
www.99designs.com.au
Pro/99designs
All rights reserved.

Edited by Sue Philips

Published by Millport Press
Printed and bound by Amazon

ISBN-13: 978-0-6459529-1-9

NATIONAL
LIBRARY
OF AUSTRALIA

A catalogue record for this work is available from the National Library of Australia

Grave Wind

CONTENTS

ACKNOWLEDGMENTS

I acknowledge my team who contributed to my book with proofreading, editing, and creative artwork. I would like to thank Momir Borocki for his illustrations that brought the book to life through imagery. Special thanks to Sue Philips for her editing and attention to detail and highlighting improvements throughout the novel.

.

P

PROLOGUE

Circa 1900

Elias Gray stumbled into the cellar. A drunken lighthouse keeper whose life revolved around the booze that did nothing to grow his reputation amongst the villagers of Solitary Island. Barely able to fit around the door into the lantern room, his bulging gut was testament to his sad existence. Enclosed with glass panels to protect the light from the elements while allowing it to shine brightly out to sea, he often crashed on the floor, only narrowly avoiding shattering the glass.

But this middle-aged man with a receding hairline and long white beard wasn't always like this before he lost his way. Remembering his days as a loving father with two children and a darling wife, he threw it all away because of his addiction to alcohol. It cost him everything, his family, his career, and his sense of purpose—he had become a tragic figure.

Flung from one lighthouse to another, he had no choice but to become a hermit in remote locations—often on his own for years on end. The maritime authorities could never find him a replacement because no other lighthouse keeper worth their reputation would move to these places. They had bargaining chips, while Elias had none.

So, he became handy for those outposts that could not be staffed by more competent lighthouse keepers. But the flip side was that the authorities left him to rot without any regard for his declining mental health and vagabond ways—nobody managed him except the monthly supply visit. And those ship captains never hung around for a drink or gave him any company—they just wanted to offload their goods and get the hell off the island. Their job was to supply the lighthouse with provisions and equipment and not to build friendships or look over the lighthouse keepers. When asked by the authorities if they found anything unusual, their response would always be, "*Yeah, he's doing alright, mate,*" they said in colloquial Australian slang.

However, there were problems with Elias Gray. When he was intoxicated on the grog, he did stupid things without realizing their consequences. He didn't deliberately set out to hurt people. Still, he would let loose on his moral values and provoke local village taboos like running naked on the beach during family outings on warm summer days. As mothers ran to their children in desperation to cover their eyes, this drunken fool flashed his genitals for all to see while making playground noises you would hear at a fairground attraction. Singing and whistling as he danced about with a bottle of whisky in his hand over a bulging stomach.

And then flirting with the beautiful local girls who despised nothing more than the site of this offending, putrid, smelly man as he chewed his words and couldn't complete a sentence. He would try everything to convince them to visit the lighthouse for tea. He seems to know all the locations throughout the island where they met to have their get-togethers—reading books, playing card games, or learning each other's dance moves. But they had become accustomed to his impromptu appearances and brushed them off by ignoring him. Usually, that was enough to send him away. The talk around the village was to not be alone when they ventured out into picnic spots, and even though he was viewed as a charming teddy bear, they never trusted him and took precautions.

"Oh, let me show you the view from the lantern room. A sight to behold out to sea and towards Vanishing Point…you can also see the passing ships at night as they signal to the lighthouse in acknowledgment of the record," he would say like a poet with one arm raised in the air as though acting a scene from Shakespear. But nobody took him seriously and laughed at him. It was entertainment value only as they politely turned their heads and walked away.

The villagers, although caught out in time, were not stupid and understood what he could do when he turned to grog. The lighthouse and its cottage became out of bounds except for one village elder by the name of Crinkled Face Joe. He kept tabs on him to make sure he was still alive. Because the lighthouse had to be operational—a kind of moral obligation to the seafarers who used the narrow, straight passage at night. Although the authorities wanted nothing to do with Elias Gray, they paid the village community a small fee to oversee the lighthouse—a kind of second eye. Crinkled Face Joe would visit Elias Gray at least once a week to chat with him and make sure everything was alright. Many times, he caught him plastered on the floor, totally out cold after a heavy drinking session the night before. He would leave the lighthouse lantern on, and Crinkled Face Joe would walk up the winding steps to the lantern room and switch it off. It was all mechanical and required manual intervention. He would then take Elias Gray to his quarters by dragging him across the cement floor, somehow managing to put him into bed. Being such a big person, Crinkled Face Joe hated the task as it required a lot of effort.

Crinkled Face Joe never disliked Elias Gray and understood he was a man with deep-seated problems. A broken-down individual who needed professional help rather than being an outcast on a remote island. The village council had raised this with the authorities many times, only to be told they didn't have anyone else capable of manning the lighthouse and that they would have to make do. Nevertheless, the caring side of Crinkled Face Joe was the only thing that stood between Elias Gray from going completely insane.

One day, Elias Gray stumbled onto something he wasn't meant to find when he lost his footing and fell down the side of an embarkment onto the old cemetery next to the lighthouse. It was a misty day, and it had been raining the whole week, making the ground slippery. It was a small and neglected grave site with around twenty headstones—most over a hundred years old. There was no caretaker for the cemetery, and the locals abandoned it unbeknownst to him.

A century of decay with gravestones leaning to the side being overtaken by the overgrown vegetation. The smaller lots were barely visible, and you must be careful not to step on the departed ones—a superstition amongst the villagers. It was the original inhabitants who were laid to rest, who had arrived two hundred years later in search of a new life. However, according to the village folklore, they brought with them a curse—a Grave Wind.

Elias Gray had fallen flat on his back, having tumbled around ten feet down the embankment. Thinking at first, he was seeing tipsy things from shots of whisky, which he believed to have found the ancient curse. Next to the headstone at the top of the graveyard, looking over the windy cliffs out to sea, he found a small cloth woven bag with its handle poking out of the dirt. He thought nothing of it at first and that it was something that the wind had carried over from one of the boats that had moored on the jetty on a windy day. And while almost ignoring it entirely, he felt a pull towards it—a radiant energy—a type of invite to come closer.

He thought his vision was playing tricks on him as he focused on the markings of the headstone, blinking many times to read it—*The man with no name*. It was the grave of the unknown, of a man who had washed ashore barely alive from a shipwreck out at sea during a storm—the only survivor.

The South Solitary lighthouse cast its beam over the dark waves, reaching as far as twenty-one nautical miles on a clear night. For sailors navigating the rugged Northern Coast of New South Wales, it must have been a reassuring sight—a steadfast friend amid the dangers of wild seas and unpredictable storms. This stretch of coast held a sinister reputation, marked by more shipwrecks than any other along the Australian shore.

One of the darkest nights in its history came when the steamer *Keilawarra*, a sturdy vessel of 964 tons bound from Sydney to Brisbane, met its fate just off the coast. A sudden collision with the *Helen Nicoll* in the treacherous waters between the North and South Solitary Islands sent the *Keilawarra* plummeting to the seabed in mere minutes, taking forty-eight souls into the deep. The tragic loss of life turned these waters into hallowed ground, which the light continues to watch over, guiding others away from the fate that befell the *Keilawarra*.

Was this the gravesite of those who perished and their bodies washed ashore, he thought.

At this moment, he recalls the tales from the villagers of a cursed breeze that sweeps through the small town of Haven's End, carrying whispers of the departed and promises of vengeance. Residents who dare to listen to the stories of forgotten sins, while those who ignore the curse are found hollowed by the secrets they sought to bury. They call it the Grave Wind, and Elias is in the thick of it.

The folklore points to a strange phenomenon, and he quickly realizes this is no ordinary haunting—it's the stirring of a Grave Wind, one that carries souls long abandoned and caught in a spiritual dilemma—many of them had not passed over.

The town's past unravels in ways he couldn't explain, confronting an evil force awakened by an ancient betrayal. But the wind has a will of its own, and the longer he stays on the edge of the graveyard, the more he senses that someone, or something, is watching, waiting, and whispering his name. The gusts of wind carried a putrid smell mixed with sea spray, condensation from the misty rain, and natural vegetation—it was a rotting stench from the dead permeating the island. As Elias Gray stood up and stumbled while holding on to the gravestone to maintain his balance, he felt a pull of energy from the cloth bag.

Should I or shouldn't I, he thought.

But curiosity killed the cat, and he couldn't walk away. He was motivated by the possibility that the cloth bag might contain a valuable item, such as gold or another unclaimed possession.

The hairs on his arm pinned upright while a radiant energy tickled his back. It was not a dark sensation that made you scream in fear but an inviting one—warm and vibrant, it felt like every bone in his body was rejuvenated. Even his knees and ankles, which had stiffened over time due to old age, felt brand new. If it was meant to be a curse from the depths of evil, it had portrayed otherwise—a lure to get him closer to inspect the cloth bag.

He felt a man rejuvenated, and the temptation was overwhelming as Elias Gray knelt onto the wet grass and damp soil, reaching out for the cloth bag—tugging it from the ground as it pulled away effortlessly from the mud. Considering the harsh elements and the number of years it had been settled in the soil, it was remarkably pristine. How it came to preserve itself in such a manner was anyone's guess, but it did raise afterthoughts.

He had never conjured the desire to look through the cemetery before, considering it was his third year on the island. Tucked away amongst the shrubs and undergrowth, it wasn't visible from the lighthouse— hidden from view just as the locals like it—out of sight and out of mind. But his curiosity led to the engravings on the tombstones.

Who were these people, he thought.

One tombstone at a time, he read the exact words, *lost at sea on the Keilawarra*. Some graves had names, while others did not. Many individuals were unidentified migrants heading towards a new destination. They would have been referred to as the graves of the unknown. But one name was clearly legible on the most prominent gravestone surrounded by the broken-down remnants of a perimeter steel fence—only afforded to families with money at the time. It was Patricia McHenry, age eighteen, and the beloved daughter of a wealthy grazing family from the east coast. Harold Mackenzie was one of the richest men in the colony at the time and owned large cattle stations and grazing land in the state of New South Wales. It would have been a family tragedy then, as Patricia was the only heir to the fortune. More importantly, father and daughter were close, and he revered his loving daughter. It is said that after hearing the tragic news, he succumbed to depression and a deep mental state—Harold Mackenzie was never the same again.

Elias Gray could do no more than reflect on what it could have been as he looked out from a vantage point on the east side of the cemetery. A reputable steamer ferrying passengers regularly before being caught in an unexpected storm. Unable to remain steady and losing control of its rudder, the ship came too close to shore and crashed into the rocks of the north cliff. The locals would have desperately tried to save them but only to retrieve bodies from the shoreline; one made it out alive—a tragedy that made the news throughout the country.

The survivor was described by locals as carrying the evil that brought the ship to its fate—possessed by unimaginable demonic foe. A pale white face with multiple facial scars and eyes that wouldn't blink. Claw-like hands and wolflike teeth superimposed the growling every time the village Elders attempted to close in on it. There was no misunderstanding that an evil curse had come to Solitary Island to prey on the locals. The people of Haven's End were devoted Christians who knew how to identify the heretic. They were not taking any chances. One night, while maintaining their watchful eye around the clock, they managed to apprehend the demon, tie it up, and place it in a small fishing boat, which they then pushed out to sea. But not before lighting the flammable oil that would combust with the added wood shavings and set it alight burning the demon—sending it back to hell. But the curse was truly gone, and the island was safe from its influence. Some skeptics would disagree and come to believe the demon had left something behind and just enough to sow the seed of evil once more.

Elias Gray wiped the mud and grass from his dirty pants that hadn't been washed for a week and headed back to the lighthouse. He smelt so severely it made no difference to his appearance and was only a habit. He was keen to open the cloth bag immediately and scour its contents in anticipation. Still, he thought it was better to determine its contents in a controlled environment. Each step up the embankment caused him to stop and take a deep breath from the exertion. The only exercise this man ever engaged in was walking up and down the lighthouse, and even then, he would keep it to a minimum. The grog had made him lazy and unfit for many chores and activities, reflected in the poor state of the lighthouse and its surroundings.

He placed his hand on his chest and felt his heart race. Elias Gray couldn't wait to turn the handle of the lighthouse entrance and take his final steps inside. And somehow, that sense of portrayal and doom that his drinking had reduced his mind seemed to fade away—like a new awakening. Everything around him felt different again.

"So, you found it," said a quiet voice in the background. "It's been there waiting for a hundred years, tucked at the base of the gravestone."

Elias Gray looked around but couldn't locate the source of the voice as he shook his head in disbelief—thinking the grog had finally rotted his mind.

"Where are you, and who are you? Or maybe you are not real, and it's only my mind playing tricks on me."

"Ha, ha," it laughed. "Oh, I'm real alright, and I am grateful that you have awakened me."

"The cloth bag?"

"Oh, it's more than a cloth bag." The gentle voice seems to come from everywhere. "It's my life in the bag…my spirit…my connection to the mortal world…unleashed and free to roam this world to your annoyance all over again."

"What do you mean to my annoyance. Are you a cursed soul?"

"Let me explain, my dear lighthouse keeper and man of the grog. A useless and tragic soul you have become." The sheer curtain flicked about as though caught in a breeze, but there was no window open in the room.

"Look outside down the pathway to the entrance to this lighthouse, and you will see what I mean."

Elias Gray took heed and peeped through the door to see a group of about ten villagers coming towards them with pitchforks and lanterns." He gulped and looked again to make sure.

"What do they want from me?"

"They are coming after you, my dear man, for what you did to that girl. And they are not taking you prisoner either?" It giggled in a squeaky voice.

"Who are you exactly?"

"I'm Betwixt. Well, that's not my real name, but it's who I have become. A spirit lost in the in-between world—half dead and half alive—I have not transitioned to the afterlife. A meandering existence I must look forward to knowing that you have released me from the cloth bag."

"And you expect me to believe that." He scoffed in a husky voice as his throat dried from the encounter.

"Whether you believe me or not is irrelevant. I don't care about what you think. But what you should be worried about is that in five minutes, that mob is going to break down that door and throw you off the cliff." Betwixt lowered its voice to a whisper as though it was talking into his ear. "Remember what you did to that girl?"

Elias Gray didn't respond immediately and then hesitated once he realized. "Oh, little Sharlene, I mean, I only asked her to come for tea, and I showed her the lantern room and the view..."

Betwixt interrupted. "A thirteen-year-old girl and underage? Hmm, apparently, you locked the door to the lantern room so she couldn't get out. What was your plan, Elias? You were drunk as a skunk and not in control of your emotions, you sexual deviant."

"No, oh no, it's nothing like that. You exaggerate."

"Do you expect me to believe that? Try saying that to that mob and see if they believe you." Betwixt snarled at him. "And those nail scratches on your arm. Where did they come from?"

"Yes, I admit she got frightened and wanted to leave suddenly, but I wasn't going to hurt her." Elias clasped his hands and dropped to his knees on the ground. "I promise on my dead mother's oath…I wasn't going to hurt her. I didn't know what to do, and when she panicked, I opened the door and let her out straight away."

Betwixt's voice filled the room as the white window sheer formed the outline of a demonic child with hands pressed upon them, creating an impression of a young girl. "This is the shape of her body, petite and with perfect contours. For thirteen years, she looked beyond her age. Attractive, I must admit, and I could see why she aroused you. She is the prettiest girl in the village by a long shot."

"It's not what you think…I'm not a sexual deviate, and I just wanted to show her the lighthouse…the view from the top."

"Ha, ha. Everyone knows you have a fetish for the young ones. The villagers made sure their daughters kept their distance from you and avoided their advances—except Sharlene, a naïve and adventurous one. Somewhat out of the mold, and you picked up on that…didn't you?" Betwixt paused and removed the contours from the sheer curtains. "Look up to the wall next to you; what do you see?."

"A rope with a noose at the end. And what do you want to do with that?"

"Yes, it's your way out of this dilemma you have got yourself into. Hang yourself now. It's better than ten pitchforks mutilating your body. Just imagine the feel of the sharp edges of each pitchfork thrusting into you one after the other—and your screams could be heard over the island. A definition of agony, wouldn't you say."

"You want me to hang myself?"

"My dear man, I don't want you to do anything. I'm just giving you a way out—I'm helping you with a pain-free suggestion. It's your choice—hang yourself or face the mob and become mutilated in the process."

In the background, Elias Gray could hear the screams of the villagers outside as they called out his name and threatened to get even. By now, they were in the vicinity of the entrance gate.

"We are not done with you, Elias!" yelled one of the villagers.

"We'll fix you. You dirty swine!" Called out another.

"You deviate.... I'm going to cut off your penis for good!"

Betwixt slid a chair from the other side of the room underneath the rope and said, "That will help you get started. Once the rope is around your neck, tighten the noose and kick away the chair. Don't worry; you will die quickly and snap your neck—be dead in an instant, and you can meet your creator. I made sure the rope was the right length, too."

"I don't believe in God. I gave my beliefs away a long time ago. When you die, that's it—you become fertilizer and nothing more," Elias Gray said defiantly.

As the collective voices of the angry villagers approached, Elias Gray looked at the heavens as sweat poured down the side of his face. He creased his forehead by squinting his eyes as his hands started trembling. His stomach curled while shivers raged through his body.

"Promise me it will be quick," he said.

"Oh yes, my dear. Quick and painless and nothing like I had to endure when I drowned off this rotten coastline. The big waves were pulling me under the reef. I was doomed the instant I was thrown into the sea by the howling wind."

"You were from the *Keilawarra?*"

"Yes, and the ship's captain also liked the grog, and on this occasion, he made terrible decisions that sent us to our doom. But how would anyone know because he went down with the ship, and the authorities blamed the storm."

The mob had reached the entrance, and with their pitchforks and shovels, they slammed their instruments on the solid timber door, making consecutive thumping sounds.

"You're done for, Elias!"

"Off with your head!"

"Wait until I get my hands on you, deviate!"

Bang, bang, bang. The entrance door started to buckle under the strain. It was only a matter of time before they would pound the mortice lock and break it.

Elias Gray walked to the chair, stomping his feet in anger. He grabbed the backrest and lifted himself upright. He took the rope and placed the noose around his neck. He kicked the chair out from underneath himself, and as the noose tightened around his neck, he cried tears and chewed his lips, knowing it was the end. The door burst open as the mob broke in, only to be confronted by the sight of Elias swinging and gasping his last breath. His legs kicked and wiggled in a nervous reaction while he suffocated. His face turned tomato red, and his tongue poked out until the last exhale.

Elias Gray was dead.

"How do we explain this?" said one of the men as he looked towards the elder with a piercing expression.

"Suicide. That's what we call it to the authorities. And we found him here hanging."

The men all looked at each other and nodded.

"Yes, suicide," they all repeated.

"And no word to anyone else about our intentions. Is that understood," said the Elder.

1

THE IN-BETWEENS

Twenty Years Later

he timber shutters rattled violently with each gust of wind like the crescendo of a masterpiece symphony, the cymbals clattering together to a climax—it was nothing more than an announcement of what was to come. An unexpected occurrence of unsettling events.

A decayed lighthouse stood on the cliff's edge, its lantern long out. The lantern room was encased in broken glass, with a powerful Fresnel lens that was the most advanced technology at the time and was now considered an old hack. The lens, now covered in dust and cobwebs, was unable to project a bright beam visible far out to sea—extinguished in the fray for relevance.

Solitary Island was located far from the mainland,

surrounded by treacherous waters that made access difficult. The weather was unpredictable and often stormy, with frequent fog that blanketed the island in an eerie silence. It was nature's way of maintaining its solitude from the quirks of civilization. The storms could be fierce, with howling winds and crashing waves. But did it matter? Not many people lived there anyway. Just a village with inhabitants caught in time and living at their own pace. It wasn't called Solitary Island for nothing.

Dahlia didn't react to the storm. She had been here before, more than once. Was she a lighthouse fan or a sucker for punishment? The jury was still out.

It was the adrenaline rush during each encounter with Betwixt that propelled her here to underscore each harrowing moment. A victory to her resilience in avoiding entrapment by the afterlife. She knew the drill because they only came out during the Grave Winds. A game of cat and mouse or do or dare. Each time, she pulled up trumps and outsmarted it only to return for more—each time elevated to a higher level—her *pièce de résistance*.

But this time, she brought with her a reluctant friend from the village who had agreed to her invitation to experience the world beyond physical realms. Dahlia had convincing ways, and Jack was a sucker for the paranormal. So much so that he developed an alias amongst the village folk: *Paranormal Jack.*

"So, explain to me what we are doing here again in this haunted place?" Paranormal Jack said. His scruffy hair and lack of attention to dress may have been misunderstood for the untidy type. But he was as sharp as a toothpick and didn't miss a beat.

Dahlia pretended to ignore him at first but realized he would only ask again.

"I told you. I come here for the game."

"With whom? I don't see anyone, just a dark, derelict room that smells like the inside of a fish tank." Paranormal Jack shrugged his shoulders while making a sniffing sound. The stench in the room was starting to affect his sinuses. "You know, the old-timers keep telling us this place is out of bounds—haunted by the ghost of the last lighthouse keeper."

Dahlia placed her hands over her mousey hair and pulled it back tightly while adjusting the ribbon.

"Isn't that more reason to come here and explore...see it for yourself? I thought you were curious?"

"Yeah, well, I am. I guess it was drummed into us as children so we wouldn't be too imaginative."

"You mean to scare us from visiting the lighthouse, Jack."

"I think some of the old timers are scarier than anything you'll find here. Right. Nothing can get uglier than Crinkled Face Joe. That scar that runs down the side of his face used to frighten the shit out of me as a kid."

Dahlia smiled. Paranormal Jack always had a way with words.

"I'm waiting on Betwixt. It always turns up during the Grave Wind."

"You mean the Grave Wind is your calling card?"

Dahlia leaned on one leg and crossed her arms. "Do you need to be so skeptical all the time? You are a paranormal guy, and the afterlife is your game. Right?" She paused for a moment and clasped her hands together. "Except Betwixt is in between life and death."

"It's called passing over to the other side," Paranormal Jack interrupted.

"Yes." Dahlia nodded. "It often talks about their frustration of not having transitioned to the afterlife."

"So, what's with the game then?"

"You'll see. It's different every time, but I expect it to be more testing than before." She walked closer to the window, which was no bigger than the circumference of an oversized man. "It usually shows itself around there."

Paranormal Jack leaned against the wall and shrugged his shoulders. "You're lucky I'm into paranormal stuff, and I know you very well, or I would have thought you'd gone insane."

The mid-summer air in the derelict room of the lighthouse, once the living quarters of light keepers, chilled within an instant. Not a precursor but a warning from Betwixt. They were ready to show themselves and unleash their curse and melodrama combined into a harrowing evil that made your worst fears look like a family picnic. Oh, make no mistake—this personified act from Hell was more than a scene; it was the real McCoy.

And no matter how many times she frequented *the time*—and that is what they called it—it did not stop a cold sweat on her back and a tingling sensation up her arms. As for the shivering—while she clutched her fists together, holding them close to her chest—that was not fear but anticipation of the next phase of the evil chapter.

Dahlia had been warned this test would be like no other. Betwixt raised it a notch to show off their strength of character. Street smarts would not be enough to carry her through the provocation this time—Betwixt pledged to get even. Was Dahlia ready for this, or had she gotten ahead of herself? Invincibility came with the territory of being a late teenager—no fear, no consequence. Cocky to the core. What could really happen to her?

"So, you're here…" It was a squeaky voice that permeated the chill.

Dahlia gulped at first before taking a deep breath. She exhaled through her mouth and captured the mist that had formed in front of her in a swirling motion.

"I see you're ugly as ever, Betwixt." Dahlia smiled.

Betwixt didn't react. It was the usual banter at the beginning of each conversation. "I accepted my fate a long time ago, my dear. The curse of identity. You know the story. I am neither male nor female, black or white, short or tall. Sometimes, my voice is deep, and other times frail. I dare not show my true form to frighten you away—because I like our encounters. It's all I look forward to in this miserable spirit world."

"You are Betwixt, after all." Dahlia moved closer to the despicable creature and pointed towards it. "Betwixt your face. It's different this time—no hair."

"What is hair but a mortal's fascination with their beauty?" Betwixt scoffed at her. "It means nothing in my world. Yes, you should try my world, if only for one day, and you could experience the horrors of a cursed death." Betwixt paused and sniffed. "I couldn't do that to you now that I have gotten to know you. But what about your friend Jack, I mean Paranormal Jack?" Betwixt hissed like a snake.

"You know his name?"

"Of course I do, my dear. I can even read his mind if I want. But that's no challenge. His mind is empty."

"What do you mean?"

"Fear has grappled him. Look at his pants. He has a wet spot on his crotch while he shakes uncontrollably. You really know how to pick them." Betwixt snuffed.

Dahlia turned towards Paranormal Jack. "It's alright. It's only a game. You'll see. Betwixt will call the challenge." Dahlia placed her hand around her mouth and whispered, "She never wins anyway." Curling her lips with a nod. "Just go along with it."

"Is it only a game?" Paranormal Jack said with his eyes wide open.

Dahlia nodded repetitiously to put him at ease.

"So, I might change the challenge now you have a friend with you." Betwixt transformed into a marionette. There were strings attached to her body, and it dangled entertainingly, tipping its hand over to gesture a welcoming advance.

Paranormal Jack thought it was amusing as he poked his head forward towards the little Mary lookalike as it pranced about, dangling on a string, inviting him closer.

"It looks so real," he said. "I want to go over and touch it."

Dahlia held back her smile, knowing Betwixt was up to no good. During her previous encounters, there was always a catch—a sideline attraction before the main event, an attempt to suck you into a false sense of security, and she was not buying into it.

"I wouldn't get too attached to it, Jack. I'd stay where you are for now."

"You're being very cautious this time," said Betwixt.

Paranormal Jack took another step forward, reaching out with his arm. "But it's harmless… I mean, what is it going to do to me?" Paranormal Jack's innocent, naive voice resonated across the room as he pointed effortlessly towards little Mary.

Dahlia clinched onto her long embroidered white dress. She felt an uncanny touch swiped across her apron like a flickering switch. Sometimes, Betwixt would get personal and let its spirit wander the room. It was one of the reasons it needed the encounters with

Dahlia to reconnect—to remember what it was like to feel mortal again.

But it was the energy of the spirit it sent out, and it could never feel again—swiping Dahlia had its limitations. If anything, it was only able to hold her attention momentarily. And truth be known, Betwixt was dead and in between the spirit world and mortal life. It had never crossed to the other side and was caught in a dimension unbeknownst to those who usually die.

As the Grave Wind ravaged outside, the high waves crashed onto the rocks below like a sledgehammer. The lighthouse was an imposing structure built from sturdy stone blocks that withstood the test of time and its elements. It stood as a solitary sentinel overlooking the turbulent sea.

The air in the room chilled even further as overspray managed to cling onto the window frame. In some instances, the droplets made their way to the floor, creating a slippery mist, just enough to send you sliding across the old rustic wooden floor if you didn't take care with your step.

The only picture frame containing a black and white portrait of the last lighthouse keeper bounced about, rattling as though it was fighting for survival.

How it managed to stay affixed to the wall was anyone's guess. But that was all part of the strange manifestations of this room and the folklore, as the last light keeper of Solitary Island had died in suspicious circumstances. And until this day, his body had never been found.

As the marionette danced, it decided on a game of trickery. It hurtled a rope that resembled a fisherman's net into the air in a circular motion, swirling toward Paranormal Jack before wrapping around him from head to toe. He was caught in a trap.

"I don't want to be tied up, Dahlia. What's going on?" He wriggled and pressed into the rope, but it only became tighter with each thrust. "Get this off me…please." Sulking as he gripped the rope, he desperately tried to pull it apart with both hands as his body became entangled in it.

"What is this, Betwixt?" Dahlia pointed to it defiantly. "Let him go or no more games…ever…I mean it!"

Betwixt responded by changing into a small three-foot doll with a puffy face and red cheeks, bulging round blue eyes, and a piggish nose. It had no upper lip with a slight dimple on its chin, accentuated by solid contours around the smallish sunken mouth. A prominent forehead and high hairline were only added to this freakish lookalike doll. Its ragged movement of the head flicked about the straight red hair to the neckline. It was like a teenage head on the body of a chubby three-year-old infant. Betwixt's dubious smile was fixed as its two buck teeth extended beyond the lower lips.

"So, do you like my real looks?" Betwixt scoffed.

Dahlia didn't respond as she continued looking away from this harrowing figure.

"Hmm, as I thought." Betwixt giggled. "Oh, this is not a game anymore. I want to raise the tempo a few notches—take away something with me this time—a souvenir of sorts." Betwixt grinned like a devil on the hunt. "And yes, my dear Jack…each time you fight the rope, it becomes tighter until every ounce of breath from your youthful lungs is exhaled, and you suffocate to death." Betwixt paused for a while and took a deep breath as though it was suffering from emphysema. You could hear the wheezing like a whistle.

"What do you mean he could die? Are you mad?!" Dahlia was outraged.

Betwixt winked sarcastically. "Oh, the games are over. My prize is watching your dear friend perish in front of you, as you are the one responsible. It was your naivety that brought him here." Betwixt lifted her fat, short arms into the air. "How does that make you feel?"

Dahlia didn't respond immediately, preferring to stave off fear. She had to think quickly. The games she had been drawn into during previous encounters with Betwixt were only a prelude for things to come. A crafty and patient build-up played by the devil's underling to scalp its prize—a human soul.

"It doesn't make me feel anything and less of you." Dahlia shifted her weight to her right leg; leaning forward, she placed her hands on her hips in a retaliatory stance.

"Oh, you don't understand the smell of death and how it consumes us. Like a drug, you know. You keep coming back for more. And each time it becomes…let's say…exhilarating."

"You're a monster…"

Betwixt shrugged its underdeveloped shoulders. "Before you, there was the last lighthouse keeper. Oh, he liked my encounters. He was so lonely that I couldn't get him to do anything. A drunken skunk at night and a deviant during the day."

Dahlia chuffed. "What do you mean?"

"He liked pretty little girls, you know until he met his fate."

"You killed him?"

"I prefer to say I took his soul and released him from his devilish desires." Betwixt grinned and nodded its head frantically. "But there were more before him… drunken fools, vagabonds, and more lighthouse keepers. They sent the rotten ones to Solitary Island…a sort of punishment by the authorities. Out of sight, out of mind."

"So why an innocent boy? Paranormal Jack doesn't fall into the profile of the victims," Dahlia said convincingly.

"Oh, maybe I didn't make myself clear. I like the innocent types occasionally. It changes things around and makes it less boring."

"You've done it before with the younger ones, haven't you?"

Betwixt held back this time, sensing she was being caught in a debate. "No need to go into explicit details, but the town records show two children who went missing and were never found twenty years ago."

"You did it?"

"They should never have ventured into the lighthouse. It was still staffed back then by cranky Bill—another drunken fool."

"You got all three of them?" Dahlia's tone turned

inquisitive.

"You could say it was a catch of the day…three souls in one night. My master certainly liked it."

"You have a master?"

"Don't we all? We're all accountable to someone along the line." Betwixt pointed to the ground. "I have no illusion that when my master is sick of me, I will end up in Hell to suffer for eternity. But for now, I amuse my master by capturing innocent souls. And that keeps me locked in the in-between world."

"Those who haven't transitioned to the other side…"

"You catch on quick, my dear. And I must say, you are the smartest of all my encounters." Betwixt paused, raised its chest, and took a gulping breath. It was the whistling sound of someone dying a slow death.

"What do you want to let him go?" said Dahlia. "State your terms, demon."

"Oh, are we negotiating now?" Betwixt scoffed at her. "A little too late, don't you think? I kind of like the boy. He's growing on me. I think he will fit in well in my world. Heck, I might even use him as a decoy to catch more innocent souls." Betwixt performed a terrible rendition of a tap dance and then stopped.

Dahlia didn't hold back her displeasure. "This is not

funny. It's not a game. Tell me what you want to let him go!" She pointed fiercely at Betwixt.

"Hmm, since you insist and care so much for the boy, here's the deal. One of you must die."

"What…"

"That is a must for my master. I must bring back a soul today. So, it's either him or you." Betwixt shook its head as the straw-like red hair became untangled.

"That's not going to happen," Dahlia said forcibly, her arms crossed over her chest in a defensive stance.

"Then you can watch him die."

The rope tightened around Paranormal Jack causing him to choke. His face turned red, and he gasped for air, desperate to stay alive. Unable to communicate, only his eyes conveyed the fear within.

"So, is it you or the boy?" Betwixt raised its index finger above its head, waving it around. "I'm waiting for an answer…"

Paranormal Jack choked even harder this time. His tongue poked out, and his eyes bulged. His face started to turn blue from lack of oxygen. "Suffocation is never a great way to lose one's life," said Betwixt. It continued to wave the index finger. "I'm still waiting…"

Paranormal Jack's head fell forward, and he began to lose consciousness. His body folded over the rope like a bird caught on a wire.

"Well, my dear, the clock is ticking… You or the boy?" Betwixt's evil rant intensified as it raised the stakes. Paranormal Jack was closer to death than ever, and Dahlia had to decide.

The Grave Wind was enraged with a thunderclap that reverberated inside the room like a giant megaphone, shaking the foundations of the old stone structure. Dahlia capped her ears with both hands. The waves were so high that droplets from the overspray landed on her nose and splashed seawater onto the floor. The room was chilled with a permeating mist, paralyzing every sense of touch. Her gut wrenched, and her feet curled as she clenched her fists and tightened her stomach. Shaking wasn't an option anymore, as she had to remain steadfast. It was a tall decision for a sixteen-year-old, even though she was mature for her age. To die or watch him die was her only choice, and each way, she would lose the battle with Betwixt. Tears consumed her as she watched her trusted friend exhale his remaining breaths, each exhale shallower and shorter—a precursor to death. Paranormal Jack was on death's door, and he only needed the slightest tugs of the rope for Betwixt to complete the possession.

"So, my dear, according to my death clock, you

have thirty seconds. Then he's all mine." Betwixt grinned with no upper lip. "You or the boy?"

Dahlia clenched her fist and shook hard. She was screaming inside as her stomach muscles tightened in knots. She wanted to vomit as she became nauseous, salivating and retching in her throat. The sweat around her forehead mingled with the chilling mist, forming droplets down her Face.

With all her energy, she turned towards Betwixt with an intimidating look—an eagle-like stare, intense, piercing, and focused. It conveyed a sense of sharpness and unwavering attention.

"Take me, take me, you monster!"

While lying on the floor in a fetal position, Paranormal Jack's eyelids flickered before opening to blurred vision. He blinked continuously to focus on the room, but it took a few minutes to get a clear view. He had passed out and was lucky to be alive.

Am I still alive? he thought. *Is this what heaven looks like?*

It soon resonated that he was in the same room as before, alone and dark. The window, the black and white picture frame on the floor—it was that same dreary grey room in the lighthouse. But where was

Dahlia?

He raised himself up on all fours like a dog while regaining his balance—shaking at first before calming down to rekindle his darkest nightmare. Although there was no rope around him, the chill in the air had returned to regular room temperature. The Grave Wind that ravaged the outside had subsided. Was it a bad dream?

As he stood up, clutching his stiff neck, he could feel the rope marks, but nothing made sense. Paranormal Jack took small steps forward and was hesitant at first before he built up his confidence again. He surveyed the room and noticed a red ribbon on the floor. It was not just any ribbon; he recognized it as belonging to Dahlia. She used it to tie her hair back in a knot.

Paranormal Jack knew this ribbon very well, and he recalled Dahlia removing it from her hair when they went fishing. She explained it belonged to her grandmother and had been passed on through the generations. He remembered how she smiled about the ribbon mischievously, telling him just enough without saying it had some mystic qualities about it.

The ribbon had words inscribed in Latin that meant nothing to him, with the year 1777. So where was

Dahlia, and why did the ribbon remain on the floor? Had Betwixt taken her as threatened, or did she run away just in time before being possessed?

But Dahlia would never leave Paranormal Jack behind, as that was not in her nature. It was a perplexing situation, as he had not witnessed what became of her. He scoured the room once more, looking for clues and calling out her name more than once, but there was nothing. She was gone.

2

CRINKLED FACE JOE

The village situated in the middle of Solitary Island had no registered name—it was known simply as "the village" or "Haven's End" because the names of places meant nothing in this tucked-away inhabitance of around two hundred people.

They were fourth-generation descendants of the original settlers who arrived on old sailing ships seeking solitude. An offshoot of a Christian cult, they came to preserve their ways and not be muddled in the lure of modern distractions. Theirs was about living off the land, the environment, purity of the soul, and God.

Every corner of Solitary Island held a secret, with unexplained phenomena and supernatural occurrences being a standard part of its lore from the outside world.

It was a place where the line between the natural and the supernatural blurred, making it a perfect setting for stories of hauntings and mysteries. Places like Vanishing Point, Silent Reef, and Forsaken Rock had the lure of being the most cursed landmarks, all with their own tales and folklore.

Strange lights—even though the lighthouse has been abandoned for decades—were witnessed by sailors and island visitors. They reported seeing its light shining on foggy nights, guiding them through the mist and treacherous waters.

Local legend told of a dedicated lighthouse keeper named Elias Gray, who hanged himself. He became folklore, which is not hard to do in a remote place where telling stories around a campfire added to the spice of the supernatural. It was said that his spirit still roamed the lighthouse, tending to its light and watching over the island. Solitary Island had all the trappings of a haunted experience for those who dared to interact with the paranormal.

Crinkled Face Joe stood awkwardly at the front of the village hall as the town folk assembled to hear his report. It had been the village meeting place for generations, a tall, steepled building that resembled a place of worship. Leaning with one arm resting on the podium, his other hand placed in his pocket, the frail older man managed to maintain his posture long enough to add some credibility.

There was a fizzle in the air, the murmurings of those trying to second guess what he was about to say. They'd all heard of Dahlia's disappearance but could only speculate on the circumstances. Rumors were rife, from a ghostly kidnapping to being pushed by a poltergeist off the dangerous cliff face at Vanishing Point on the other side of the island. There were also the mysterious caves near Silent Reef, designated out of bounds by the Elders. Everyone had a story to tell and an opinion. Until they heard it from Crinkled Face Joe, it was nothing but hearsay and village talk.

"I apologize for bringing you all out on a cold night for an important announcement," he said with trepidation. He placed his hand gently across his lengthy white beard, caressing it as an icebreaker that seemed to calm him a little. Public speaking was never his forte, and he preferred the other Elders to communicate announcements such as these. But this one belonged to him—the paranormal had been his responsibility for decades, and no other Elder dared tread on his toes.

"You've all probably heard about Dahlia's

disappearance. I want to give you an update on our recent search of the island." Crinkled Face Joe took a deep breath to maintain his composure and paused while looking across the room. Groupings of families were all dressed alike, with the same hairstyles that appeared lost in time. From an outsider's perspective, it was as though time had no meaning, and progress was just a distraction. Why make changes for the sake of it when everything is working fine? The villagers were not tainted by developments of the mainland—it was the purity of soul that dominated their value system, being true to yourself and your fellow villagers. They were one giant support mechanism to each other.

"We have sent out a search party to look everywhere—the fishing spot Dahlia frequented, the dark caves, the keeper's cottage, the lighthouse, and the jetty... Nothing...no trace of Dahlia." He forcibly pointed directly towards the entrance. "But I know she is out there—somewhere not of this world—another dimension."

"Is it the curse of the lighthouse again?" called out a skinny, frail man, raising his hand timidly while clinging to his suspenders.

"Brother Jonathan, the curse of the lighthouse is folklore. You know that. Local legend tells of a dedicated lighthouse keeper named Elias Gray, who hanged himself. It's said that his spirit still roams the lighthouse, tending to its lantern while watching over the island."

Chatter broke out amongst the villagers as they all looked at each other, waiting for someone to challenge Crinkled Face Joe's response. The story of Elias Gray was a touchy subject that flirted with claims of his hauntings and curse—it made them nervous.

Jonathan stood up in an assertive stance—folded arms, head upright, chin pointing forward as he tightened his lips in frustration. He was not taking the usual jibe from Crinkled Face Joe this time.

"Since I was a child, you have been telling us the same story—to stay away from the lighthouse because it's cursed. And it bothers us that you didn't tell us why. We all know the story of Elias Gray, who committed suicide. We did the same thing today—we sent a search party and found nothing. Yet, the tourists keep coming to the lighthouse on their paranormal adventures for their fright night, and you do nothing to stop them despite the dangers."

There was a round of applause from the villagers as Jonathan's point of view resonated. Renowned for being outspoken, it did not come as a surprise for

Crinkled Face Joe.

"Brother Jonathan, we don't own the lighthouse. It belongs to the national trust, and tourists are allowed to visit. We are paid a fee for the upkeep of the property and to ensure the tourists are reminded of their own safety and obligations. But we are not a principality, and we don't own the island. We don't make laws. We only control our ways and our values—how we choose to live and bring up our children."

"What about Forsaken Rock? Have you looked there?" called out a woman as she raised her arm.

Crinkled Face Joe paused before he responded. Forsaken Rock had always been a touchy subject in the village folklore. "The weather was not kind to us, my dear, and we weren't able to reach there—but we are planning to search Forsaken Rock as soon as the weather improves."

"We know she liked to go there to look over the island at its highest point," said the woman.

There was quiet in the hall. The villagers seemed to give up hope as they got the same rhetoric from the Elders. One by one, they stood up from their chairs and made their way out of the hall quietly, without fuss…except for Paranormal Jack, who felt a tap on his shoulders—it was Crinkled Face Joe.

"Hello, Jack… We never really got to talk in detail about Dahlia's disappearance, but I have a question," said Crinkled Face Joe.

Jack acknowledged by lowering his head slightly, hesitant about making eye contact. Crinkled Face Joe may have spoken to him only once before, but Paranormal Jack preferred to keep him at a distance. And like most of the villagers, he was frightened by his presence, a sort of mystique while growing up in the village.

"Yes, what would you like to know, Mister Joe?"

He smiled gently, accentuating the deep scar down his face—a reminder of why many of the villagers felt uncomfortable around him.

"Did you see the demon?"

Paranormal Jack took a moment to respond. "Yes, but Dahlia had a name for it—Betwixt."

Crinkled Face Joe stayed silent for a moment. "Hmm, she really said that?"

"Yes." Paranormal Jack nodded. "More than once."

"And you haven't mentioned that to anyone?"

"No, just you, Mister Joe."

Crinkled Face Joe shuffled his feet restlessly and then looked him straight in the eye. "I want to let you in on something, and only because you're a paranormal guy." He gently placed his hand on Jack's right shoulder.

"The village Elders are the only ones who know the demon's name—Betwixt. But we don't tell anyone or talk about it. For generations, we have kept it a secret, and as far as the villagers are concerned, it's the ghost of Elias Gray. I mean, the villagers must believe in something, right?" Crinkled Face Joe removed his hand from Paranormal Jack's shoulder and placed it on the straps of his farmer's overalls. "Do you understand me, boy?"

"Oh yes, Mister Joe. I got it. I know how to keep quiet."

"Yes, I know. You've never been the outspoken type—introspective and keeping to yourself. We rely on those traits to share this information with you."

Paranormal Jack didn't respond, patiently waiting for Crinkled Face Joe to make another revelation.

"When I was a lot younger, I was the paranormal guy in the village. They made fun of me, thinking I was off with the fairies. But little did they know that every generation has one paranormal person in this village, and we have been overseeing you since you were a child. The Elders know you have the spiritual connection—the gift to see the afterlife."

Paranormal Jack decides to be bold and speak out as frustration builds inside him. "I don't know if that's a gift or a curse, Mister Joe." He lifted his head to make eye contact. "So, what happened to you when you were the paranormal guy? Did you ever see Betwixt?"

"Hmm, you ask hard questions, but they're fair. I guess you have a right to know, considering what you have been through."

"Know about what, Mister Joe?"

"About my face—this terrible scar that has left me deformed. It happened during a confrontation with Betwixt."

"At the lighthouse?"

"Yes, in the exact same room where we found you, where Dahlia went missing." Crinkled Face Joe took hold of Paranormal Jack's arm and held it tight. "I was lucky to get out alive. But I can't say that for my cousin Eldred—consumed by the demon, his soul captured for an eternity." Crinkled Face Joe held back tears as the memory of his cousin came rushing back to haunt him. "I went to the other side, you know—the in-between world, they call it. Only some of us can crossover—the ones with paranormal abilities." He looked Paranormal Jack straight in the eyes, expressing hope. "Like you, my boy, and you're the only one in the village who has the same connection with the spirit world."

Paranormal Jack tilted his head slightly with a puppy dog's innocent stare, "Can you tell me more about the in-between place? If you feel up to it, that is…"

Crinkled Face Joe looked around to make sure there was nobody nearby to overhear what he was about to describe, then took a deep breath and nodded reluctantly.

"I've never been asked that question before—to describe my experience, to relive the pain. I spent years trying to suppress it. Nightmares, and waking up in cold sweats followed by anger and then anxiety. You see, the trauma lingers on. A scar that won't heal, except it's inside your head, and your shadow speaks to you."

Paranormal Jack wasn't sure if he had overstepped his welcome by poking into Crinkled Face Joe's ordeal with the afterlife. But at the same time, it was not he that had raised the topic. He had been invited to listen to the older man's tales. He thought he was being polite to a village Elder renowned for his fragmented personality.

"At first, you're not sure if you are awake or asleep,

and you struggle trying to grasp what state you're in. That causes immediate confusion as to what reality you occupy. You hope it's a bad dream, that you'll wake up soon, and it'll all be gone. But that is not the case, and you start to think about death and whether you died in your sleep." Crinkled Face Joe took hold of a chair nearby and pulled it towards him, preferring to sit down while he recollected his thoughts.

"And what happened then…?"

"Yes, curiosity killed the cat, my boy. You have an inquisitive mind." Crinkled Face Joe crossed his legs and tightened his lips, knowing the next part was where the horrors lay. "Darkness fills the room—pitch black, and you don't know what is up or down, left or right. A sort of place that makes no sense. Until…" He paused and faced Paranormal Jack with a hawkish gaze. "Until they find you, and it's not a welcoming party either. Their objective is to take your soul and then send you to the ravages of Hell."

Paranormal Jack twitched a little, wiggling his eyebrow. "Who are they? Demons or monsters?"

"Hmm, that's inventive of you, my boy, and you are close. What if I told you that your worst nightmares begin to ring true? A race for your spirit, and in my case, it was Betwixt. A demon who is not a fully-fledged *cacodemon*—an exiled evil spirit who struggles with its identity. A confused and perplexing poltergeist."

Paranormal Jack realized this conversation could drag on, so he pulled over a chair and sat in front of him. He placed his elbows on his thighs, holding his hands together and resting his chin on them. From a distance, he looked like he was praying, but he was only making himself feel more comfortable.

"At first, Betwixt was polite, asking me to join them in the afterlife—a precursor to the abduction of my soul. But I didn't fall for that trick. This angered Betwixt, who realized it had to make good work of it. I was going to be a tough catch, like an overgrown marlin caught in a fisherman's net fighting to break free."

"Did it threaten you after you refused?"

"Oh, it was more than a threat. It was the uncontrollable anger of a beast from Hell as it growled so loudly while spitting venom and cut across the stomach with its five-inch nails in an act of self-mutilation. A despicable act that we mortals would find confronting. But in my opinion, it suffered no pain from the self-inflicted wounds. I was told it was an example of what it would do to me if I refused—rip my stomach open and spill my guts out in front of me."

Paranormal Jack gulped from the expressive detail as he tried to imagine the extenuating horror.

"And weren't you horrified by the thought?" Paranormal Jack lifted his head directly in front of Crinkled Face Joe to force a response.

Crinkled Face Joe shifted his posture by moving to the side and placed his hands around the back of the chair, turning his head away from Paranormal Jack.

"Hmm, I feared you would ask. What is fear other than a reaction to impending doom? Would you believe me if I told you that your fears in these circumstances take on a different context? You become more attentive to the environment in case you need to fight back." He clenched his right hand into a fist. "And fight back, I did, in every way I could."

Paranormal Jack nodded and didn't say a word as he waited to discover the pinnacle of the confrontation.

"There are two things I always carry with me everywhere I go—my holy cross and a small amount of holy water. These blessed representations of God's spirit are an enigma for every hellish creature. The holy water is like acid to a demon, and they can smell it from a distance. The cross you wear around your neck, which is blessed by a priest, emits a powerful energy that immobilizes them. None of these instruments will destroy a demon, but they will give you enough time to get out and run." Crinkled Face Joe paused for a while, gathering his thoughts as he gently rubbed his hand across the scar along the side of his face. "See this...the demon gouged my face with its claw and there was venom that prevented total healing...scarred for life."

Paranormal Jack, sensing reluctance, triggered the next part of the story. "But something went wrong, didn't it?"

"Yes, my boy. Not everything went to plan." He shook his head. "And for the first time ever, I encountered a demon who was immune to both the sign of the cross and the holy water—it had no effect on the beast from Hell."

"And what happened after that, Mister Joe?"

"I managed to come back to the physical world and don't ask me how. Something pulled me back—some type of energy. I thought I was doomed to the depths of Hell."

"I suppose that's where it all ended?"

"Hmm, not so fast, my boy." Crinkled Face Joe took another deep breath. "It didn't end there. I was plagued by nightmares, waking up with cold sweats reliving those harrowing moments in my dreams—a kind of aftermath as though Betwixt had messed with my head."

"It visits you in your dreams?"

"Betwixt can tap into your thoughts and cross over into your dreams when you are at your most vulnerable—in a deep sleeping state." Crinkled Face Joe pointed to his temple with his forefinger. "This is where it comes after you eventually to torment you."

Paranormal Jack paused and waited for Crinkled Face Joe to gather his composure. "And what did you know about Dahlia's powers?"

"She was a rogue psychic who had paranormal abilities, but far beyond anything we could imagine. I don't think she understood her capabilities." Crinkled Face Joe gulped and swallowed. "She was difficult to contain—a mind of her own, and adventurous to the point that she continuously put herself at risk." Crinkled Face Joe placed his hand on his chest as he felt his pulse. "It was not the first time she had been confronted with evil. We knew she was playing games with Betwixt and foresaw problems."

Paranormal Jack nodded. "You got that right. Dahlia had a strong personality and was stubbornly steadfast. Nothing seemed to frighten her." Paranormal Jack became confident enough to probe further. "But did you ever raise your concerns with her?"

"Oh, she never told you the times we summoned her to the Elders for a meeting. More than once, we advised her to be careful and to not take advantage of her paranormal abilities." Crinkled Face Joe scoffed, throwing his arms in the air.

"No, she never told me anything about these meetings..."

"We informed Dahlia the demon would play on her feeling of invincibility—entrapment, we called it. By creating an environment that makes you come back for more...a sort of addiction." Crinkled Face Joe moved his head towards Paranormal Jack, so close that their noses nearly touched. "I have a proposition for you, and the Elders have agreed. Are you interested?"

"Is it about getting Dahlia back? A plan?" Paranormal Jack's eyes lit up with reborn enthusiasm.

"That will be part of it, but there is a bigger picture at hand that I need you to consider first." Crinkled Face Joe took a deep breath and placed his hand on the back of the chair for support. His aging body and slight hump to his posture meant he was barely able to support himself upright for extended periods. This feeble older man who should be using a walking stick refused to succumb to the frailties of a body in decay.

"The keeper's cottage adjacent to the lighthouse, my boy. The small, abandoned house that once served as the lighthouse keeper's residence."

"The place you have been telling us since I was a child to stay clear of—that bad things happen to those that dare visit the place?" Paranormal Jack couldn't wait to make a point of the contradiction.

"Yes, I knew you would raise that point. And there was a reason for it—to keep you all safe from Betwixt."

"And it was kept secret from the village folk for all these years?" Paranormal Jack stood, took a step back, and placed his hand on his forehead in a reflective mode. "For generations, you told no one about Betwixt and instead treated us like fools not capable of understanding the evil that resided in that place. So, you made up stories to draw on our emotions—you drummed up the fear."

Crinkled Face Joe didn't respond straight away, preferring to stay silent as he looked outside to the forest to gather his thoughts. He stood up, placed his hands on both of Paranormal Jack's shoulders to comfort him, and nodded.

"I understand how you feel, Jack. The younger people of the village are different from my time. We did as we were told and never questioned anything."

He was saddened by the thought that most villagers would come to realize the Elders had lied to them about the lighthouse and that it would be his legacy—not telling the truth. As previous generations went about their business without questioning anything, the younger people of the village today, like Paranormal Jack and Dahlia, were a new group of teenagers who questioned things—curious to the core.

And even though Solitary Island was an outpost of civilization, people from the coast visited the island—paranormal investigators who came to garner their thrills from the haunted lighthouse. Each time, they mingled with Paranormal Jack and Dahlia despite the Elders' request to stay away. A sort of cohort to learn more about the island and its hauntings while acquainting them with new ways from the mainland—a type of exchange.

And even though the lighthouse and the lightkeeper's cottage were in disrepair, with broken windows and an overgrown garden, they had become a tourist attraction because of their eerie reputation amongst psychic mediums and paranormal investigators. Many came hoping to catch a glimpse of the ghostly keeper or experience the strange phenomena themselves.

"I understand I have given you much to think about, my boy, and it was not the type of conversation you thought I'd have with you. Heck, I barely spoke to you in the past, and this must have come as a surprise. There's a lot to take in, and I get it." Crinkled Face Joe caressed his long white beard more than once and sighed, relieved that he was able to get it off his chest.

"So, you really meant it. You want me to join you in confronting Betwixt at the keeper's cottage at the next storm," he said.

Crinkled Face Joe looked up to the sky and breathed in through his nostrils. "I can smell a storm coming; it could be sooner than you think." He looked Paranormal Jack in the eye with a piercing stare. "What do you say? Are you up to it? Want to bring Dahlia back?" He clenched his fists together and held them tight. "Remember the risks, my boy, and what happened to me. You need to think carefully about the horrors that await you. Are you prepared to take down this demon like I did?"

"Only this time, we are wiser. We have your experience to draw upon. And I know Betwixt's tricks in advance." Paranormal Jack didn't hold back his youthful enthusiasm.

"Yes, and I'm an old man. This could be my last

time to face off with the treacherous beast—perhaps my time has come."

3

THE GRAVE WIND

J*ack walked briskly through the dense* forest along the pebble rock pathway that led to the keeper's cottage.

It was a short five-minute walk from the village that had been used for over a century by the locals—the only quick access to the lighthouse. It was fanned by tall pine trees on either side that had grown to a height that sheltered daylight and the sun-like a canopy. If you wanted tranquility, shade from the hot summer months, and coolish temperatures, the dense forest was a place to be. Along the pathway, you can see evidence of how the villagers accommodated the natural environment by building resting places from fallen logs and small areas cleared of vegetation. A type of resting zone for the mind—a place to go to reflect and calm down if need be. All the villagers found their way here eventually to cry away their problems to find they cleared their minds. Was it a type of natural therapy or one of the mystics of the island?

He moderated his intensity so Crinkled Face Joe could keep up. A mix of youthful enthusiasm and anxiety had gripped him as they made their way to face off with Betwixt at the keeper's cottage. Paranormal Jack had never been inside the keeper's cottage as it was designated out of bounds by the locals. All except for Dahlia, whose trademark was to break the rules. Apparently, she had told him about her exploits in that place. A story of a harrowing escape from an evil poltergeist—although she was known to exaggerate her evil encounters when in Paranormal Jack's company.

"Not so fast, my boy...I don't have that spring in my step like I used to."

Paranormal Jack turned his head to find Crinkled Face Joe falling behind and gasping for air. He stopped and waited for him, not wanting to be disrespectful to the older man. Breathing heavily and clutching his hips, Crinkled Face Joe looked like he was about to collapse as he grasped Paranormal Jack's arm.

"I think we should take a breather for just a minute," he said, red-faced and huffing like a goldfish.

Paranormal Jack found a fallen log that must have come down during the last storm and sat on it, hoping Crinkled Face Joe would follow suit.

"It's coming, you know."

"What is, Mr. Joe?"

"The Grave Wind." He pointed into the horizon to a gap between the forest and the shoreline. Dark cumulus clouds formed as a cold front headed for the island.

"You mean a storm, don't you?"

Crinkled Face Joe turned his head and said, "The Grave Wind is not a storm. It's a curse….an evil entity."

"I'm sorry, but I don't understand Mr. Joe."

"Every so many years, it makes its way to the island, bringing along unimaginable horrors. The Elders know about it, and we take precautions for one night as it passes through. We tell the villagers to prepare, and they all know the drill."

"But I don't remember the last time it passed through?"

"No." He nodded. "Too distracted to remember. But for me, it was like yesterday. Unfortunately, when it arrived ten years ago, two children went missing that day at Vanishing Point. Never to be found." He paused and continued taking deep breaths as his body readjusted to a regular pulse.

"You're talking about the Johnstone twins?"

"Yes, the two beautiful fifteen-year-old daughters of Marcus Johnstone—he's long gone now, but at the time, it devasted him and broke his heart—we all felt the pain in the village."

"I was too young to remember when it happened, but one thing for sure is my mother always attended the anniversary of their death at the Johnstone's home." Paranormal Jack went quiet for a moment and then decided to change the topic as he was enthused by the Grave Wind.

"Can you tell me more about this Grave Wind? That's something we were never taught about in school."

"It normally embeds itself in the lighthouse, but it has been known to frequent the keeper's cottage, Vanishing Point, Forsaken Rock, and Silent Reef."

"Is that how those places got their names? I always thought about why there were such morbid descriptions for the island."

"Yes, and over the past century, bad things happened at those places. Ask any of the village folk, and you'll find someone who has been affected by the loss of a loved one."

Paranormal Jack looked from the corner of his eye and tilted his head slightly. It's what he usually does when he is thinking. A curious posture for someone who was in a reflective mood.

"I'm a little confused, Mr. Joe. How do you know the difference between a storm and the Grave Wind? It all sounds and looks the same to me. Perhaps one big storm over another and nothing more…. coincidence, maybe, or folklore. As villagers, we like to make up stories."

"Huh! Always testing the boundaries, and that's your skeptical side talking."

"Is that a bad thing?"

"No, not at all. I hope I didn't come across as being condescending. You should always test the things people tell you, particularly about the supernatural. I admit that some stories are made up and exaggerated. They make good village yarns. But the Grave Wind is real, my boy and only those with paranormal tendencies can tell the difference."

Paranormal Jack shook his head. "And I still don't understand how you can do that. I mean, decipher the differences. A storm is just a storm to me—dark clouds, wind, and rain—nothing more than that."

Crinkled Face Joe stepped toward Paranormal Jack and took a seat on the log. With his hands firmly placed for balance, he turned to him and said, "Close your eyes and tell me what you smell in the air; take all thoughts out of your mind and connect with the nature around you. Breathe in and out gently and listen to your body's rhythm."

Paranormal Jack took a few minutes to adjust his body rhythms to the reflective technique. "The air has a taste about it I can't describe very well."

"But are you tasting air, the physical elements of the storm, or are your senses reacting to something else?"

"It doesn't smell like a storm, is what I mean. The smell of moisture, the frigid air that comes with it. It's as though it's touching me like a gentle vibration with a humming sound in my ears."

"Look at the hairs on your arm."

"They're standing upright," said Paranormal Jack. He was caught by surprise.

"But you're not shaking from the cold air and no goosebumps." He tapped Paranormal Jack on the shoulder. "Now look at me from the corner of your eye, and what do you see?"

He tilted his head slightly while looking at Crinkled Face Joe from the corner of his eyes. And while it took a while to adjust, he became perplexed.

"So, what do you see, my boy?"

"Your hands are covered in a soft glow. It's a trick of nature. That's all it is."

"There's your skeptical self again being dismissive. But I don't blame you for that because that's the way we are taught to conform with our surroundings."

"You mean we only see what we want to see?"

"I would rather say that our brain has taught us to see things conventionally—we play by the rules, so to speak. We block out at least seventy percent of what is around us. In a way, we have become insular without realizing it." Crinkled Face Joe smiled as he threw in a little banter. "Look from the corner of your eyes at the tree in front of you."

Paranormal Jack did what he was told, and he became enthused. "Same thing, a gentle yellow glow."

"Now look into the horizon directly at the storm and tell me what you see."

"Storm clouds heading this way, but wait, everything in that direction has no gentle glow. In fact, it feels…"

"Feels like what?" prompted Crinkled Face Joe.

"Morbid, a dull energy. It feels terrible and irreversible."

"You can see a storm, smell it coming, and feel the temperature drop. That's nature's way of letting you know that it's on its way. But can you feel the energy of the storm? That's the Grave Wind, my boy. An energy of evil that uses the storm as a carrier."

"It rides the storm?"

"No, it comes with it. It's the evil storm that brings misery, death, and horror to anything in its path."

"So how do you know all this, Mr. Joe."

"Oh, I was taught by a village Elder before me. Everything is passed down, you know." Crinkled Face Joe paused to gather his thoughts and gripped his hands. Something he always did out of habit when he was about to say something important.

"You're testing me, aren't you. To see if I have the same paranormal qualities. To feel the evil energy of the Grave Wind."

There was silence as both came to terms with the task at hand. Crinkled Face Joe stood up and caressed his long white beard. "Yes, I have been waiting for the Grave Wind to see if you have paranormal abilities. It was always part of the plan, you know."

"It's why you brought me here?" Paranormal Jack's shoulder-length hair flicked into his face as a gale hit the shore, signaling the arrival of the storm. He stood up and looked down on Crinkled Face Joe. His lanky posture and skinny frame that supported his six-foot-two height made him one of the tallest villagers. With a slightly pointed nose and a square jawline, his face looked more mature for his age than an eighteen-year-old.

"Here, take this ribbon and hold it when you're in the keeper's cottage," said Crinkled Face Joe. "Never let go of it."

Paranormal Jack gently rubbed his fingers over the silk fabric and said, "It's the same ribbon Dahlia had with her before she disappeared at the lighthouse."

"Yes, and if I am right, it's saved her soul from the demon."

Paranormal Jack took the ribbon and looked at it closer, examining the design. "It has an inscription, but I don't understand it."

"It's an ancient language from our early settlers, my boy, but it is now long lost to the villagers. Only some Elders can decipher it. Powerful words to ward off evil, but it also has a form of energy about it."

"I don't feel anything."

"It will come in time. Your mind is not attuned to it—invisible for now."

"Like the glow from the corner of my eye?"

"Yes, you need to train your mind to accept it. But I can help you with that…it's how I was taught by my Elders."

Paranormal Jack continued rubbing the ribbon gently, expecting an immediate reaction, but he felt nothing.

"You said before that Betwixt is affected by this ribbon, but I still don't know why a monster like that can't fight against its energy—holy water does nothing, and the cross can't contain it."

"Why the ribbon, you ask?" Crinkled Face Joe placed both arms on Paranormal Jack's shoulders and lowered his head slightly. "Close your eyes and concentrate on the ribbon. Keep rubbing it gently with your fingers, but don't force it. Feel the softness of the fabric and the warm energy. Let it come to you slowly, and let down your guard…make yourself vulnerable."

"It's an energy unlike anything I have ever felt before—calmness, confidence, and kindness—I feel protected like someone is holding my hand."

"And what else can you feel?"

"Positive energy. It blocks out anything from the other side—evil, bad things that make you unhappy. A sort of peace." Paranormal Jack smiled radiantly. "I could hold it forever."

"That's good, my boy," Crinkled Face Joe whispered. "It's the energy of generations all bottled up into one ribbon. Of Elders who came before me. The words on the ribbon are sacred and not meant to be spoken out loud."

Paranormal Jack was in a hypnotized state as the energy of the ribbon continued to absorb him.

"But we need to go to the keeper's cottage now," interrupted Crinkled Face Joe. "The Grave Wind is almost here, and I feel the presence of Betwixt."

He patted Paranormal Jack on the shoulders gently to disassociate him with the energy. Rain drizzled through the forest canopy as droplets touched their noses. The gale hit the shoreline as leaves swirled violently. The pine trees shook from the violent wind gusts. But there was also an eerie quiet. As though nature was conscious of the storm, it had a different tempest than the usual spring rain that battered Solitary Island yearly. The rain smelt like a mystic powder blended with the natural fauna. And in the distance, there was the sound of crashing waves on the rocks below.

Crinkled Face Joe grabbed Paranormal Jack's arm firmly and said, "We need to go to the keeper's cottage now!"

"It's there?"

"Yes. But look at me. Once inside the cottage, it will help if you do everything I say. Don't try to interpret the situation yourself. It's dangerous, and Betwixt already knows your vulnerability from your previous encounter."

"It will come after me," Paranormal Jack said as he swallowed.

"No, both of us in a form of trickery. It will attempt to hold the weaker one ransom first." Crinkled Face Joe stopped in his tracks and eagle-eyed Paranormal Jack. "It will be dangerous, unlike anything you have ever seen before. Make sure you have your wits about you and don't try to outsmart it—you're not ready for that." Crinkled Face Joe paused for a moment. "Do you understand me, Jack?"

He nodded reluctantly. "And Dahlia?"

"We're going to get her back." He clenched his fists tightly. "Because evil is arrogant and stupid. It would help if you looked for weaknesses. And have a strong sense of awareness while exploiting gaps. Stay calm under pressure so your mind is not obsessed with fear.

"That's easier said than done," Paranormal Jack said reluctantly. "I lack your experience."

"Hmm, look and learn by watching me. Hear every

word I say and watch my movements."

4

THE KEEPER'S COTTAGE

As they neared the rusty steel gate of the keeper's cottage; Paranormal Jack dreaded the horrors awaiting inside.

With overgrown weeds, a slanting tiled roof, and visible cracks in the walls, the cottage should have been condemned. On the mainland, the house would have been demolished. Years of neglect had turned this Victorian-era building into nothing more than an eyesore.

The only thought that managed to take his mind off the encounter with Betwixt was the smell of sickness in the air. Behind the cottage was a small cemetery that was used by the original inhabitants of the island. That, too, was also left to rot into the ground with falling tombstones and overgrown weeds. It was where the curse of the Grave Wind was believed to have originated.

With each gust of wind, the putrid smell permeated up his nostrils and deep into his lungs. He understood why it was different than the winter storms that pelted Solitary Island this time of year. He placed his hand over his mouth, wanting to vomit as his stomach spasmed with each breath. It was like gasping for air in a pool of deep water, drowning and unable to touch the bottom on tiptoes.

"Oh, don't worry about the smell, my boy, that will pass," said Crinkled Face Joe as he placed a bandana over his mouth—he was better prepared. "It's the tip of a storm front and just the beginning."

"It gets worse?"

Crinkled Face Joe didn't respond, preferring to take his mind off the putrid odor by pointing to the cottage. "Do you feel anything unusual?"

Paranormal Jack took heed to his question and looked from the corner of his eye. "No glow…the cottage has a dead feel about it. Morbid."

"Hmm." Crinkled Face Joe nodded. "Correct, there's no life in this cottage anymore. Any distant memories have long gone. Any semblance of happier days and lightkeepers going about their daily routine traded off for the evil within."

"You mean Betwixt?"

"Bad things happened in this cottage over the generations—one light housekeeper after the other, they all perished by way of self-inflicted wounds."

"Suicides?"

"The villagers call it a curse. Men who lost their minds." He placed his arm on Paranormal Jack's shoulder and patted him gently. "That's what we prefer to call it—mental health issues brought about by the solitary confinement of this outpost—not to mention the lonely existence. The ones they sent here were at the bottom of the barrel as far as lighthouse keepers were concerned. The unwanted ones—drunks and some with a fetish for children—if you know what I mean." He cleared his throat by making a grunting sound. "They had no friends or families and didn't mix with the villagers, but I should rephrase that by saying we encouraged the villagers to not mix with them. And I suppose that didn't help with their isolation either."

"When growing up, we never spoke about the keeper's cottage only to be told it was out of bounds. The word amongst the town folk was it had a poltergeist—it was cursed."

"The curse of an old lighthouse keeper—Elias

Gray?"

"Yes, that's right—Elias Gray."

Paranormal Jack realized this was the moment to raise the curse.

"I will let you in on something never to be repeated to anyone in the village." Crinkled Face Joe had a serious look on his face.

"You know me, I'm not a chatterbox type, Mr. Joe."

"He didn't disappear. That's a story made up by the Elders back then. They created the folklore of the ghost of Elias Gray to divert the villager's attention from the horrors of this lighthouse. Before you say anything, I disagreed with the decision at the time because it created a haunting that was misleading. Instead, we glorified Elias Gray and the story of his ghost that haunts this lighthouse—supposedly. Well, at least that's what the tourists from the mainland think."

Paranormal Jack placed his hand over his forehead, surprised by the revelation, and sighed while still gasping for breath from the Grave Wind. "How did he die?"

"Hmm, a tragic death. He hanged himself just over there." He pointed to the lighthouse steeple just beneath the lightbox. "Naked and with his hands tied behind his back. And the most curious thing is he died with a smile on his face as though a deep burden had been lifted from his soul. All the suffering of mental anguish—the man had gone mad and become dysfunctional. But death freed him from his pain.."

"In retrospect, shouldn't the authorities have relieved him of his duties?"

"That's a good question, my boy. The inspector from the main island was aware of his plight. Still, his visits became infrequent. Constant excuses are either bad weather, lack of transport, or lack of resources. They didn't care about him. As far as the authorities were concerned, he was a problem that couldn't be resolved. They had nowhere else to assign him, and nobody wanted to come here."

"The authorities put it in the too-hard basket?"

Crinkled Face Joe nodded but remained silent as he looked out over the shoreline. He raised his head, sniffed twice, breathed in forcibly, and closed his eyes momentarily.

"Betwixt is here. I can sense it."

"The energy, you mean?"

"It's in the cottage. It knows I'm here, and it's waiting for us. It recalls the previous interaction with you. It considers you a soft touch…easy prey."

Paranormal Jack gulped and clenched his fists.

"The demon's coming after me?" He turned back towards the pathway leading out from the cottage. "Maybe I should leave while I still have a chance."

"Unfinished business from last time, my boy. It made a trade-off with Dahlia, and you got away. This time, it wants to get even, and it wants you."

"I'm not going in there!" He was startled by the revelation his life was in danger.

Crinkled Face Joe leaned on the side of the gate to maintain his balance. "Whether it's here or somewhere else, the Grave Wind will find you. It could be Vanishing Point, Silent Reef, or Forsaken Rock—it has you in its sights. And if you don't confront it now while I'm here to protect you...you don't stand a chance."

Paranormal Jack's right hand was shaking as he felt a tingle throughout his body. His stomach muscles tightened while nervously tapping his right foot. His eyes watered while tightening his lips and grinding his teeth. He felt as though the world had crashed down on him. To be told he had to fight the demon to survive had sent his emotions into panic mode. The pure horror had absorbed him.

"Are you ready to go inside?" Crinkled Face Joe had seen it all before, and it reminded him of his first encounter with Betwixt.

Paranormal Jack did not respond immediately, preferring to turn his head away while folding his arms tightly around his chest.

"Remember what I told you before…don't react to its trickery and lies. I will do the talking and make sure it doesn't go for you first." Crinkled Face Joe spoke louder. "Did you hear me, Jack?"

The storm ravaged along the rocks of the lighthouse, sprucing spray like a jet stream high into the air. It was situated on the outermost point of the island. From a distance, you would have thought it was on the edge of the sea and surrounded by water, but that was an illusion of the rising terrain that led to the building.

The sea spray that filled the air was carried by gusts of the Grave Wind. And it didn't smell like salt water mixed with soft rain. It had a stench that made your nose wrinkle, and your lungs expel air quicker than you could breathe it in. The body rejected the putrid redolence and somehow knew it was wrong for you.

The only light bulb that provided a flicker of light to this dark outpost struggled to keep a constant glow as it phased in and out. It was driven by a battery that was old-hat technology. It had never been updated despite continuous requests to the relevant authorities.

Even though they were happy to take the fees from the tourists visiting the lighthouse, the island levy was never re-invested back into Solitary's Island infrastructure. The villagers always had a disdain for the mainland authorities, and rightly so.

They slowly walked up the path to the keeper's cottage, trampling sticks and crunching leaves beneath their feet. Their legs scraped along overgrown shrubs and thick ground cover vegetation poking small holes and tearing into their jeans. What was once a beautifully maintained stone pathway was now a muddy black dirt track taken over by the forces of nature. Paranormal Jack held onto Crinkled Face Joe's arm, frightened he may lose his way. Being tossed about by the gale and the torrential rain sliding off his face, making visibility impossible. He rubbed his eyes continuously like windscreen wipers, only to have to do it again.

"We are here, my boy," said Crinkled Face Joe.

They made it to the front door of the cottage, a thick timber door made of the most robust wood on the island.

"How do we get in?" Paranormal Jack was eager to get out of the storm even though he knew of the horrors that awaited him inside.

Crinkled Face Joe pulled out a bunch of old skeleton keys on a metal ring. It was a mortice lock, and as they dangled, he knew which key fitted perfectly into the lock, turning as it disengaged with a loud click. He then pushed the door open with the palm of his hands, stepping aside for a rush of stale air to exit the building.

"Nobody has been in this building for years," said Crinkled Face Joe, still wearing his bandana over his face.

Nobody frequented the cottage because it was cursed and haunted by the spirit of Elias Gray. Even though tourists had full access to the lighthouse, this building remained permanently shut. A testament to the power of the evil curse over the century, so much so that even the authorities on the mainland were not prepared to restore and open this infamous cottage.

Crinkled Face Joe turned to his right and switched on the main power, which was still active considering its age. Back in its time, the electricity generated in this facility was state-of-the-art technology—ahead of its time and built to last. But not now, it was barely functional.

He paused for a moment and looked straight ahead towards the room where he last confronted Betwixt.

Memories come rushing back in a sinister way. A gentle glow filtered through the gaps in the door as an orange hue laced the walls in perpendicular themes. It was a reminder that past horrific encounters don't always go away. We are taught to categorize them in our minds on the premise we don't revive them. But some triggers make them come back, reliving the pain and anguish that made them in the first place. At this moment, Crinkled Face Joe had to face off with his demons again.

"Are you alright?" asked Paranormal Jack. He could see Crinkled Face Joe was in a predicament.

He looked down and closed his eyes just for a moment while he caressed his scar gently with his fingers, not in any meaningful way but as a remembrance of what evil can do to a person on a given day.

"It's been a long time since I have been in this situation, and the memories run deep. Flooding in like a series of still pictures telegraphed across my mind," he said. But he then raised his head high and was resolute. Crinkled Face Joe was impervious to the dangers that awaited within. "All the more reason why I must confront this poltergeist and bring Dahlia back."

The door in front of them suddenly flew open, bouncing off the walls like shutters in a storm.

"It's angry," said Crinkled Face Joe.

Paranormal Jack stood there, not saying a word.

"Because it didn't finish me off last time, and now it's going to be three times harder. It's got its work cut out."

Paranormal Jack pointed at the door and nodded hesitantly. "Do we really need to go in there? I mean, I can wait for you here?"

"Just stand behind me at all times and follow me."

The illumination intensified, and the door battered violently against the timber frame. Strange voices of spirits trapped between spirit dimensions started filling the room. Some words made no sense at all and were more akin to growls and hisses—a baritone and squeaky pitch with the underlying timbre of a child's voice all merged. It wasn't very clear to decipher the messages.

"I can hear Dahlia," said Paranormal Jack.

"You can hear her amongst that squabble?"

"Yes, Mr. Joe, she's asking us to get her out."

"She's really saying that?" He turned his head with his ears facing the room. As Crinkled Face Joe was partially deaf in one ear, he used his better one to home in on the voices. "You must have some special hearing powers to decipher dead voices, my boy, as I can barely get a fix on her."

"Oh no, she's trapped like the others, but only she has the psychic ability to connect with us."

And while voices of the dead continued to talk over each other like a mishmash of undecipherable words, they stepped into the living quarters where Elias Gray once lived. They placed their hands in front of their eyes to block out the blinding glow as they waited for Betwixt to appear from the clearing mist.

"You're still into making grand entrances," said Crinkled Face Joe. Betwixt's image appeared where he'd expected, next to the porthole-like window. It was reinforced with exterior steel, making it more bizarre how the demon was able to slip through the rusty metal rods.

Betwixt scoffed as though something was caught in its throat and said, "I see you brought the boy with the empty mind," Paranormal Jack had been pre-warned of its emotional tactics designed to extract a reaction. But he heeded Crinkled Face Joe's advice and said nothing.

"We want the girl back—Dahlia. You took her, right?" said Crinkled Face Joe. He was not pulling any punches and went straight for the jugular.

Betwixt growled incessantly, realizing its words had no effect. "You like to cut to the chase, old man." It slithered its red tongue like a king cobra snake and turned sideways, levitating about one foot off the ground. As it toggled its tiny toddler-like legs, the body's disfiguration became more evident. Words could not explain this beast; such was its ugly appearance.

"Very funny, but we aren't here for your magic tricks. The show's over," said Crinkled Face Joe.

"You could at least laugh. I haven't done that trick for years." Betwixt regained its posture and stood straight. It was a small dwarf-like creature, not more than four feet tall.

"I have a deal for you, old man. Let's swap the girl for empty head over there." It raised its arm, pointing a crooked finger at Paranormal Jack. "I think the girl was a bad choice. She has become too hard to handle— too independent and won't take orders—too rebellious. And an empty head over there will do what he's told and will be much easier to manage. So, what do you say, older man? Do we have a deal?"

Crinkled Face Joe took a candle and matchbox from his jacket pocket. The first attempt to light the match failed as the wild wind outside permeated through the cranks in the cottage wall, making it harder for him to light a flame. He wrapped his hand around the matchbox this time and tried again. His shaky hands didn't help as the next attempt split the match into two.

"Are we going to be here all day? Third time lucky." scoffed Betwixt. "And what are you lighting up anyway?"

Crinkled Face Joe managed to maintain his discipline and lit the match, placing it over the tea light candle. He immediately put the candle on the floor in front of Paranormal Jack. The incense was familiar to him—frankincense, myrrh, benzoin, and cedar used in the village chapel during Sunday mass. He lit another candle and placed it next to the first, creating a half-circle barrier.

Betwixt was caught by surprise while the incense appeared to distract it momentarily as its distorted mouth coughed while struggling to cope with the fragrance.

"This type of witchcraft isn't going to help you, old man," said Betwixt.

Crinkled Face Joe turned to Paranormal Jack and said, "Can you communicate with Dahlia?"

"Yes, we're connected by thought."

"Tell her to come towards the incense as it will penetrate the dimension."

"She said she can smell it."

"Good, I'm going to put my hand through the energy source connecting with her dimension. Tell her to grasp it tightly so I can pull her out."

Crinkled Face Joe knew where to locate the entry to the dimension, the *in-between* world, guided by the white vapor of the incense swirling in circular formation toward the gate to the spiritual entrance.

He took several cautious steps forward with his arm extended towards the spiritual entrance. Betwixt rubbed its eyes viciously and continued coughing uncontrollably. The anger inside manifested in a rage as the door behind them slammed shut. An oppressive force tried to push Crinkled Face Joe away from the spiritual entrance.

He gritted his teeth and squeezed his lips, forcing against the negative energy. His eyes shut as he concentrated all his efforts by thrusting himself one step at a time. He grunted and moaned as he struggled to make ground against evil. He was not going to give up against the demonic foe, as every inch gained became a victory.

Betwixt became angrier, shapeshifting into a seven-foot monster, a demon with two horns, standing on hooves like a wildebeest. Its red eyes permeated like a laser light in a show of intimidation. It growled by raising an octave each time to rattle their nerves. Its wolflike teeth protruded outward, dribbling green slime like an angry dog to accentuate its prowess. The anger generated heat that exuded from its metaphysical form, causing steam to rise from its armpits and ears and into the chilling cauldron that the room had become. It was playing with their minds to suffuse an apprehensible fear.

Crinkled Face Joe reached into his top pocket and pulled out a ribbon identical to the one he'd given to Paranormal Jack. The two ribbons together will create stronger protection as well as double the ancient force, enabling Crinkled Face Joe to succeed in extracting Dahlia from the in-between. His hands were shivering from the moisture in the air, and he tried desperately to overcome the profuse climatic state as he quivered.

"Call out to Dahlia. Do it, Jack, and tell her to seek the energy of the ribbon…"

Paranormal Jack tried desperately to maintain his composure against the repulsive demon who had its eyes set on him—a prized scalp of the one that got away. Betwixt was not going to let him go so quickly this time. He wanted to rush out screaming as bitter memories of his previous experience engulfed him. Still, he tried to remain resolute—he didn't want to leave Crinkled Face Joe and Dahlia behind—that would be gutless.

"She can feel it…oh, oh, she can see you now." he stuttered, barely capable of putting a sentence together fluently.

Betwixt was not just a shapeshifter and a demonic foe that could change climatic conditions at random. It was a repulsive and unforgiving poltergeist with a singular goal to get its way. Anger was a ploy to intimidate and drive fear into the mortal souls of those who dared to confront it.

It was caught in a dimension of the spirit world for an eternity. A prison cell without metal bars and high-security doors. We are taught of only three places we go to when we die—heaven, purgatory, or hell. But another dimension sits *in between*—with one hand bouncing off the physical realm and the other caught in an endless motion that is nothing more than a revolving door taking you nowhere. There are no visible exit points. An intense dark space with no sense of gravity or direction—worse than your most horrific nightmare.

Objects flew across the room as they ricocheted against the stone walls. Anything that Betwixt could elevate, such as old picture frames, a wooden chair, and a small mirror, became part of its demonic prop. An action-orientated expression designed to make you panic and flee. The antique side table rattled forcefully, lifting one foot off the ground before falling back onto its four legs with a loud thump.

The negative energy continued to fight against Crinkled Face Joe as Paranormal Jack was being pulled upwards and could barely keep his feet on the ground. Ducking instinctively from the airborne objects directed towards him, it was only a matter of time before he succumbed to a fatal blow.

Crinkled Face Joe had managed to penetrate the invisible vortex as Dahlia clasped onto his hand. He was present in another dimension while the other continued to fight against the torment of Betwixt in the physical realm. And while he'd partially crossed this time, it felt different. He understood that to save Dahlia, he would not return to the spirit world to complete the exchange. There was one thing Crinkled Face Joe didn't mention to Paranormal Jack, which was the rules of the game. For one spirit to cross into the *in-between* dimension, one must come out. It happened to him when he last fought Betwixt many years ago. To get out, someone had to take his place, and it was another Elder from the village who had saved him.

"Jack, I'm pulling Dahlia out…but…"

"But what, Mr. Joe?"

Crinkled Face Joe turned towards Paranormal Jack with a penetrating look. Paranormal Jack knew what it meant when someone said goodbye for the last time.

"You're not leaving us, Mr. Joe?"

There was a pause in his response, and then he unleashed himself. "Now, take hold of Dahlia's other hand when she passes through! Pull and pull until she's out. And Jack—both of you get the hell out of here while I confuse the demon!"

There was a tug of war as Dahlia's hand penetrated the dimension—first her hand and then her arm. She was off the ground, vertically. Such was the force behind her trying to pull her back in. Paranormal Jack did what he was told. He gripped her hand, leaning back as a counterweight and tugging with all his might.

Agh, agh, he sighed as he continued his extraction. Crinkled Face Joe had been pulled into the other side and lost to the spirit world. His physical outlines had turned into specs of matter undistinguishable from the human eye. Dahlia had broken through as the demon lost their grip on her. Laying on the floor mesmerized and unsure of what she'd been through, Paranormal Jack lifted her onto his arms as they made their way out of the lighthouse.

"What about Mr. Joe," she said.

Paranormal Jack didn't answer at first, preferring to get her out of harm's way. He kicked open the door and carried her down the cobblestone pathway to the iconic rusting gate.

"Mr. Joe is gone—an exchange for your soul." He sat her on a log outside the gate—an old fallen part from the tall eucalyptus tree that was a landmark of the original lighthouse.

Dahlia shook her head a few times as she came to terms with her new reality. She had crossed over and returned to her own dimension, leaving behind an experience built on horrors that she would later recount. But it came at an expense—a tradeoff that was voluntarily taken by Crinkled Face Joe—an older man making his last hoorah. He knew how the system worked. Nobody came out of the *in-between* without someone pledging their place—those were the rules he kept to himself for so many years.

Betwixt was powerless in this instance as it was also bound by the rules. And if Crinkled Face Joe took Dahlia's place, there was nothing it could do. A soul for a soul was always considered a reasonable outcome by the underworld. And someone as influential as Crinkled Face Joe was a major prize for the demonic overseers of this terrible place.

As Paranormal Jack and Dahlia looked back at the keeper's cottage, they saw a brilliant yellow glow that seeped out through the gaps in the door and window sills. Pulses of light that pushed out in straight lines like the rays of the sun momentarily and then ceased. It was over, and Crinkled Face Joe was gone.

There was more damage at Haven's End as the Grave Wind ravaged through the island and into the village. Although the villagers had become skilled at managing the cursed wind, there was always something or someone who would be affected in strange ways. All they could do was minimize the damage of the evil gust as it permeated through the island in search of its never-ending retribution. Nature's intelligence had found that it could form part of the evil this island possessed. Taking on a form of spirit not usually associated with climatic events.

A wind with an evil spirit in search of its own victims? Or possibly unable to control its momentum and intuition—not intelligence but a tool for evil to cast on the unforgiven and innocent one.

5

LADY JANE BRIGHTON

I t was rare for dignitaries to visit Solitary Island, and this time, it was a surprise.

Rumors amongst the villagers were rife about the arrival of Lady Jane Brighton. The word was out at Haven's End. A tip-off from one of the sailors who had a slippery tongue. Constantly seeking attention, this sailor, known for his big mouth and loud personality, couldn't help but mention it while unloading goods during a previous stopover. And for an island whose only communication was word of mouth, this sailor played an integral part in spreading the news.

Lady Jane was an Australian third-generation descendant of British royalty but without the accent. Her family was not aloof and had humbly settled with their wealth. They rarely flaunted their money and preferred to stay under the radar—unnoticed and without fuss. With all that wealth and privilege, she did not display a pompous attitude. Amongst her circle of friends, she was considered to have blended in too much with the commoner. However, Lady Jane was somewhat of a non-stereotype and anti-establishment—not afraid to voice her opinion. Regarded as outspoken on specific issues about the land. So, what does someone like Lady Jane do when you have everything?

The answer to that question may lie in the simplicity of life itself. Lady Jane had lost her only child at the tender age of ten in a freaky accident. Her son Harvard had drowned in a nearby river when the rope snapped from a branch, propelling him into deep water. It was the usual play area where children would go for a dip during the hot summer months, except he couldn't swim. Too far from the river's edge, his friends tried desperately to save him—but they couldn't reach him as he got pulled away by the current. By the time word got out at the mansion nearby, he was floating downriver, with his head facing into the water and his body like a log. It was a stillness that meant only one thing during these tragic events. It tore Lady Jane apart and drove her into depression. The pain and the agony of losing a loved one tormented her, and up until now, she never gave up searching for him in the afterlife.

It was her mission in life to find a way to communicate with her dead son. Lady Jane had always been into the mystique and curiosity of the spirit world since she was a child. She always believed that death was a transition into an afterlife and that our inability to accept a world beyond death prevented us from communicating with the dead. We had created our own barriers and conditioned our minds from early life. Her view was that we were not taught to expand the possibilities of our senses. Trapped in a perimeter that prevented the use of our potential.

For many years, Lady Jane tried every avenue available to reconnect with her son before she stumbled upon her psychic abilities. Even as a child, she could see things in people that others could not. With some training from a psychic medium, she was able to connect with the spirit world. The love for her child forced her to open the part of the brain we all keep locked up and suppressed, as well as our ability to see over and above our narrow existence. She exploited our potential to reconnect with her child.

Lady Jane discovered that our ability to connect

with the spirit world was a gift we all had chosen to ignore through conforming behaviors. From a very young age, we are taught to comply, but you can't do this. And exploring beyond commonly accepted conventions was frowned upon. It was like putting a padlock on that part of the mind.

She was convinced there was a life beyond death. Whether that was an energy or spirit existence, call it what you like; death was not the end but the beginning of a metamorphosis to a new life. She knew this because she had heard his voice and touched the spirit energy of her son on many occasions. It gave her comfort knowing that Harvard was not lost forever and that one day, they would reunite.

I'm fine here, mummy. Don't worry about me. I'm here with Uncle George. Her son would say in a gentle voice that would send a shiver up her spine.

Her exploration of the outer realm of the spirit world brought her to Solitary Island and the haunted lighthouse. Word had spread amongst the psychic fraternity on the mainland about the mystery of the Grave Wind and the story of Elias Gray. She wasn't the first psychic to visit the island either. Many mediums had come before her, seeking evidence of the afterlife. Some gave up after being tormented, and they couldn't deal with the evil energy. Others had claimed to have encountered Betwixt in a sinister game and the entrapment of the evil shapeshifter. Betwixt didn't care who you were as long as the game was palpable with an opportunistic bent. Unperturbed by these events, Lady Jane wanted to see it for herself: a world where life and death meet in a head-on collision—the *in-between*.

The seaman unloaded Lady Jane's belongings off the transit ship that made the voyage every week from the nearby coastal port. Her affluence was captured through branded luggage. Dressed immaculately with the finest attire and accessories—she was a lady of the times. As she disembarked from the ship, one man standing tall in a dark suit and top hat made a point to watch her every move—he was her bodyguard and personal assistant. One would argue why she needed someone like him, but it was commonplace in those days amongst the wealthy.

He directed orders on her behalf to the ship's crew as they sought advice on where to place her belongings—a list of ten large suitcases—but there was one small black bag she kept close to herself. Tightly secured with a padlock and made of the finest crafted steel with silver embossing—it was no ordinary possession. Her name was engraved on the front side in gold embossing—*Lady Jane Brighton.*

Dahlia looked towards Paranormal Jack with a cheeky grin while soaking in her arrival.

"She's so pompous," she said while flickering her index finger in a royal salute.

Paranormal Jack couldn't help but laugh it off as he tugged her gently. "We'd better be on our best behavior; it's our job to take her to the lighthouse cottage—remember?"

"You know I won't go in that room, Jack. I'll escort her to the front gate, and then it's over to you." Dahlia placed her hands on her hips in a commanding manner.

"That's the routine, alright, and there's nothing to be worried about." He reassured her like he did with every visitor. It had become a constant theme with new arrivals, leaving the living arrangements to Paranormal Jack while she stood back and watched.

"But what if she asks me to personally show her around the keeper's cottage." Dahlia paused for a moment. "You know I don't feel comfortable about going in there after all these years."

Paranormal Jack took hold of her hand and looked her straight in the eyes. "I told you I will handle it,

Dahlia, like we always have."

Dahlia and Paranormal Jack had matured and were in their early twenties by now—many years had passed since their encounter with Betwixt and the loss of Crinkled Face Joe. However, they always promised not to let the demonic presence defeat them—a form of rehabilitation to show their spirit had not been conquered by their past encounter with the shapeshifter. As far as they were concerned, the battle with Betwixt had never concluded but had taken on a different meaning. It was an ongoing standoff between good and evil to dominate the island.

They stepped down the last flight of stairs that led from the pathway to the entrance of the jetty, making their way towards Lady Jane. It was the same pathway that had been used for over a hundred years, covered in low-lying shrubs and with thick bushes on either side. A reminder this was Solitary Island, an outpost off Australia's east coast.

By now, the transit ship had offloaded all the goods into wooden crates and was ready to set off back to the mainland. Mariners had long thought the island was cursed, and it was common for them to leave immediately. They were a superstitious lot, and they knew the story of the island.

The story of Elias Gray had become folklore, bound by a mistrust of anything to do with the lighthouse. Some sailors preferred not to step onto the jetty for fear the curse of Solitary Island would capture their souls and unleash bad fortune. Others thought the mysterious Grave Wind would engulf them if they arrived on the island at the wrong time. They constantly checked the wind's direction and the smell in the air—two signs that the Grave Wind was on its way. With the curse so well known, it meant fewer sailors would sign up for the trip as the shipping company struggled to replenish its labor.

Lady Jane notices Dahlia walking towards her while Paranormal Jack struggles to keep up. Wearing white leather gloves worn only by the wealthy and a symbol of her excesses and family fortune, she waved her right hand.

"Good morning, Lady Jane. I'm Dahlia, and this is my good friend of many years, Jack…but everyone calls him Paranormal Jack." Dahlia said confidently. She waited for a reaction, unsure whether she was required to curtsy or not.

"Oh, my dear, no need to kneel before me. I'm not the queen," she smiled. "And haven't I heard of you both? Your reputation precedes you, Dahlia—the spirit hunter and your protegee, the infamous Paranormal Jack. What a dynamic duo you both make." She extended her hand for a handshake. And before she released her gentle grip, she closed her eyes for at least five seconds."

"I feel your pain, my dear, and your spiritual energy. You have seen the afterlife, haven't you? I sense it."

Dahlia let go of her hand. "I have been to the *in-between*, a place where life meets death, an intersection to the beyond, where good and evil are in a constant battle for domination."

"You're not afraid of dying…are you," said Lady Jane in an impromptu manner. Her voice exuded confidence.

Dahlia nodded but was silent at first.

"Well, tell me, dear. What is it like?" Lady Jane sensed her reluctance and unease and then paused. "It's fine, my dear. Bad timing on my behalf. Maybe next time we talk about our experiences." She winked and smiled. "I have so much to share with you also—about the afterlife, that is."

Lady Jane turned her attention to Paranormal Jack, not wanting to appear rude, and extended her hand. He was unsure at first, as he had never met anyone like Lady Jane, let alone touched the hand of the gentry.

But deep inside, he thought, *oh, what the heck*, and he gripped her hand for a firm shake. Dahlia followed suit with her trademark smile.

"You are both so young. And you, my dear," she said, turning to Dahlia. "Are a catch for any man. What a pretty thing you are."

The tall man, standing over six foot two inches, gave the sailor his orders. He walked up beside Lady Jane and nodded.

"We're all done, Ma'am."

"This is Mr. Gordon. He is our family administrator and looks after our business affairs. He's here to make sure everything goes according to plan," she said with a grin, pointing to the lighthouse. "This island does have a tragic history, so you never know, and it is best to have the security of one of the best men in the land. Mr. Gordon was my father's choice many years ago before he passed away. He's loyal to our family, and if there is anything he needs, your cooperation would be helpful."

Mr. Gordon tilted his head, avoiding the sun in his eyes. He squinted and blinked as though he had a twitch. Paranormal Jack thought he may have a nervous disorder at first but soon realized he was struggling with the elements. Mr. Gordon was not a man of the rough but of sophisticated bearing who should not be underestimated. With an illustrious background in the Royal Navy and rising to the ranks of a commander, he managed to prosper later in life with his skills and reputation. It helps when you're associated with the wealthy.

"Can you show me the way to Lady Jane's quarters? Oh, and can you give a hand with her luggage, my boy?" he said in a deep, commanding voice.

Paranormal Jack hesitated at first and glanced at Dahlia. "Yes, of course, but only one at a time. Those bags look heavy."

"Put some muscle into it boy…lanky lad like you shouldn't be a problem." He looked at Paranormal Jack from head to toe while pursing his lips. "You could do it with a bit of toughening up, lad."

Lady Jane smiled to ease the tension in the air. "Don't mind Mr. Gordon; he's always like this." She turned towards him and smiled. "We can be polite to our guests, Mr. Gordon. I'm probably the first aristocrat they've ever met. You don't want to make them feel uneasy or think badly of us."

"Apologies Lady Jane. I won't be so tough on the boy then…they're only villagers, after all." He smiled at Paranormal Jack and said, "What about the room then?"

"We don't go into that room anymore. We had a bad experience there some time ago. But we can take you to the keeper's cottage and open the door for you." Dahlia interrupted, dangling some old keys on an ancient keyring. "Oh, and don't worry, we have a villager who is responsible for the upkeeping of the guest room. There is everything you need inside—fresh produce from the village—eggs, fruit, vegetables and dairy."

"Lady Jane does not cook for herself," said Mr. Gordon forcefully.

"Lady Jane would have been made aware that the stay at the keeper's cottage does not include catering." Dahlia was not having any of his arrogant talk. "It's not a hotel but a remote stay on an isolated island.

Lady Jane did her best to shrug off the interjection. "It's fine, Mr. Gordon, the girl is right. There is no catering provided; we'll have to rough it a little." She smiled at Mr. Gordon and then added, "You remember your days in the navy when you were sent on missions into dangerous territory—I guess it's something like that."

"Oh yes, like the mountains of New Guinea or the coast of the Falklands. You're quite right, M'lady."

Despite Lady Jane's opulence, she was also capable of going without and taking on the role of an adventurer. She'd had to do it in several remote locations she'd visited while exploring her connection with the afterlife. Solitary Island was not her first journey to rediscover that connection. She had visited other remote places on the Australian continent. In towns where there was evidence of a spiritual connection with the afterlife, Lady Jane would explore the potential to bring her closer to the borders of life and death. A sort of tipping edge into the unknown.

Mr. Gordon had taken the room in the lighthouse, away from Lady Jane and the keeper's cottage, which was a separate structure. The lighthouse keepers back then had a choice of sleeping in the keeper's cottage or the lighthouse, depending on the circumstances. That really came down to choice. However, in the original design, it had more to do with being on hand during a storm. Many visitors to Solitary Island preferred to stay in the lighthouse because it was rumored to be haunted by the ghost of Elias Gray. It was about the experience and adrenaline rush of chasing a ghost that had become folklore. However, someone like Mr. Gordon, who was not into supernaturalism, wouldn't have known about the haunting and frankly wouldn't care. For him, it was just a room like any other, although it was a little below his usual standards.

Mr. Gordon placed his coat on the chair and made sure it was sitting perfectly with no creases. Before sitting on his bed, he patted it with his hand like slapping someone in the face gently to flick away some white specks. He checked the bedside table for dust by wiping his forefinger across it before setting down his items, satisfied with their cleanliness. He sat on the bed, bouncing a few times to check the mattress for comfort and squeaks before leaning forward to remove his boots. He took a deep breath, knowing that his lower back would ache a little from stooping forward. It was all part of the aging process as far as he was concerned—the aches and pain synonymous with growing old.

It was a long journey from the mainland to Solitary Island, and he was tired. Serving as Lady Jane's personal security attaché was demanding. She always needed something, and it kept him on his toes, but it was draining, to say the least.

"Oh, don't get too cozy, my man." A voice hustled in the background.

Mr. Gordon thought he was dreaming at first as his

eyes partially closed until he heard the voice for a second time. He jolted up and reached for his pistol next to the bedside table. He looked around but couldn't see a thing that would conjure a voice. The room only had a small portal-type window the size of a ship's cabin.

"Show yourself!" Mr. Gordon exerted forcibly with an authoritative tone.

"You won't find me anywhere. I'm in between this and that. Caught in no man's land, so to speak."

Mr. Gordon stood up, aiming his firearm. He was prepared to discharge it as he methodically moved around the room like a tiger on the prowl. His military instincts had kicked in, and he was in fight mode.

"Like I said. You won't find me anywhere unless I'm prepared to show myself. But for now, you will have to settle for my voice."

"Show yourself, or I will shoot!" he shouted.

"I'm already dead, so shoot at what?" the poltergeist laughed. "Shooting me would make no difference other than make yourself feel better." It laughed again, but in a satirical manner this time.

Mr. Gordon continued circling the room while pivoting from a stationary position.

"So, I have a madman in my midst…"

"I'm not a man or a woman…I'm Betwixt, and I can be whatever you want me to be. A cat or a dog…but my favourite is a half-manikin and half-child monster. Gruesome if you ask me, but it's the one that has the best effect on those stupid enough to venture into this lighthouse." Betwixt scoffed. "And I have sent many fleeing in fear from this room. They thought they could handle Elias Gray's haunting. Thrill seekers that call themselves ghost hunters or psychics."

"So, what do you want from me?" said Mr. Gordon directly. He wanted to get to the point as he was not a man who liked to mince his words.

"Ha. Ha. I was waiting for that. I will give you a choice…straight up as you wish."

Mr. Gordon kicked the mantelpiece in frustration and raised his voice. "This is not a negotiation. Show yourself, you coward."

"Now, now. No need to get personal. We barely know each other. But let me offer you an opportunity to get out of this quandary you're in."

Mr. Gordon didn't respond and remained quiet, preferring to keep his anger from spilling over.

"See that rope with the noose hanging from the ceiling. That's for you."

"Huh. You want me to hang myself, you crazy son

of a bitch."

"Like I said, there is no need to get personal. This is what I do for a living. Or not living depending on which way you look at it." Betwixt paused and took in a deep breath that sounded more like a vacuum-sucking air. "Well, you may have no choice. You see, I know you killed Lady Jane's son, didn't you? You're the one who cut the rope from the tree while he was swinging. Oh yes, you hated being bossed around by him—a little rich boy with a bad attitude who was spoilt and treated you like his servant. And there was nothing you could do about it. Either put up with it or lose your very generous salary and conditions."

Mr. Gordon spat on the ground. "How dare you accuse me of that. What evidence do you have? You are neither here nor there. Remember?"

"Oh, we have a witness. Someone who never came forward. A teenage girl who happened to be on her way to the creek witnessed you cutting the rope. And you threatened to kill her if she said anything. Pointing a gun to her head." Betwixt dropped the tone of its voice to a whisper. "You don't remember."

"You think you're so smug. How are you going to organize a witness to report it? You're a poltergeist, aren't you? You don't exist—an in-between. Your words, not mine."

"Would you like to take a chance on that? She's arriving on the next boat with the police inspector. It's all been arranged. You're going to be arrested, and your name will become mud."

There was dead silence as Mr. Gordon retreated to the bed and sat with his head bowed. His hand trembled, and his leg shook as though he had a twitch.

"So, what do you say? Hang yourself now, and nobody will ever know. I will make sure that the ship never arrives at the jetty. We do have terrible storms in this area that come without notice. Many a life was lost at sea, and ships sunk in these treacherous waters. Failure to comply will result in arrest and prosecution, where all evidence will be presented before the court. You will make all the headlines as the controversy ignites the minds of the public with huge interest. Everyone will come to know Mr. Gordon as a murderer of children."

"You're an evil monster of the worst kind—whatever you are. You will pay for this."

"Oh, you can't bully me, Mr. Gordon. I'm not your average person that can be pushed around. I'm out of reach. To top things off, they will find the knife in the river after a deep search to back up the eyewitness story.

Yes, it's still there after all these years thinking it would never be found." Betwixt paused for a while and laughed sarcastically. "You forgot you dropped the knife in the flurry when you were caught by the girl?"

Mr. Gordon looked starry-eyed at the noose hanging from the ceiling just in front of him. His eyes flickered as he contemplated his death at the hands of Betwixt. It was either die or be shamed for life. A man with a prestigious army record and revered among the wealthy elite of the country. His family name stood to be ruined and become mud for generations.

"What are you waiting for. I don't have all day, Mr. Gordon. Make a decision….die and keep your name intact or ruin your family line." The voice echoed in a mocking tone.

Mr. Gordon stood from the bed, steadfast, looking into the abyss. He was a military man and familiar with the last moments of life. Having seen soldiers in their dying moments on the battlefield. Death was no stranger to him. But he was a man with pride and dignity who would not allow shame to overcome his family name. He had made his choice, but it would be expressed in actions and not words. He did not respond to Betwixt, ignoring it altogether.

Mr. Gordon walked to the noose looming menacingly above his head. He stepped up onto the chair and placed it over his head. He had made his decision as he placed the noose around his neck and stood on the chair. He had a staunched look and wanted to show no fear.

"If I'm going to die, it will be with my head held high," he said.

He clenched his fist and tightened his lips as crease marks around his eyes became deeper. His stomach churned in apprehension. In his last moments, he adjusted his tie and tucked his shirt around his waist. He flattened out his hair by making sure it parted to one side. If one were to end one's life, it had to be proper—like a gentleman.

He kicked off the chair holding him in position, and dangled, kicking instinctively while he lost his breath. Suffocating to death, his face turned red, and his eyes bulged out until he came to rest. Mr. Gordon was dead.

6

THE GHOST OF LYDIA GOW

Tubular bells rang unexpectedly in the town of Haven's End at sunrise, echoing a feisty sound at regular intervals.

Most of the town's folk were having breakfast, so it came as a surprise. It meant something of significance had happened and that the townsfolk should congregate at the town hall to be briefed by the Elders. Although it disrupted their routine, it provided a sense of awe—something was up, and they were intrigued. The usual course of action was to drop what you were doing and make our way to the town hall, but many couldn't help but snaffle a couple of pastries along the way. There was no rule against eating at the town hall. By this time, Dahlia was out in the field gathering herbs for her recipes. It was her pastime. Although not officially trained, she gained her knowledge from the village Elders, who passed it down through generations.

Herbalists seek to find the root cause of illnesses. They choose herbs based on the symptoms or ailments a patient describes during the consultation. They would also perform an assessment, inspecting certain areas of the body and creating a personalized prescription, for which Dahlia had no hesitation in being at the forefront of providing remedies. Her patients would use just one herbal treatment or a combination of herbal supplements, depending on the nature of their diagnosis.

Typical forms of treatment included making teas, capsules containing liquids, or using powdered herbs to make up bath salts, oils, skin creams, and ointments. Dahlia had become the point of reference to help villagers with their ailments with perfectly prescribed remedies that usually worked—or at least they thought it would—it was the placebo effect, or they just worked.

She placed her gatherings into her tote bag, which separated the different plants into smaller packages with digging tools and snippets. It was a short walk to the village center over a small ridge. Her thoughts had shifted to what the news could be. Without trying to pre-empt the announcement, nine times out of ten, it was terrible news associated with the lighthouse or the impending arrival of the Grave Wind. But very rarely does she ever recall positive news, and she often wonders why the call by the tubular bells had become synonymous with negative announcements. The villagers of Haven's End had become conditioned to thinking such negative thoughts.

For a quiet village like Haven's End, the announcement brought everyone out of their usual habitat. Suddenly, a stream of people flocked from everywhere to the town hall. Soon, you realized the actual population of the smallish town and how everyone looked alike—dressed the same and even spoke in a dialect more aligned with old English—and, to some extent, Shakespearean talk.

The building was the only structure in the village made of stone. It once served as a residential administrator's office- until it became too expensive to continue providing that service from the mainland. Converted into a town hall, it served many purposes for the villagers and Elders, who had also transformed it into their central office. Like a small-town shire, the building had several functions, one of which was to help the community of Haven's End with a variety of services. And if all the villagers were present, the size of the building was barely enough to hold everyone in, occupying every corner of the small hall to get a view.

It was organized so that every family had their unofficial spot, making seating arrangements more manageable. Even though they weren't numbered and marked, somehow, the villagers found their way through the crowded room in an orderly manner. Dahlia usually sat just behind Paranormal Jack near the front of the room so they could trade signals about the quality of the communication. They had established a basic type of sign language over time that nobody could decipher. It looked odd from a distance, but it seemed to work effectively for them.

An older man with scruffy hair, a long white beard, and a pointed skinny nose stepped up onto the slightly elevated stage. He was flanked by two other Elders who resembled him—a kind of image for the town executive. Wearing a long black coat with a ceremonial gold chain bearing a holy cross, it was the only form of chivalry the town had passed down from their original settlers. For a society that didn't prize precious metals and stones, it may have been seen as a contradiction to outsiders.

The Elder cleared his throat and raised his hand, calling for silence. As he tried to clear the phlegm in his throat, his airways gave way to a wheezing sound as he struggled to regain his breath.

"Brothers and sisters, I have important news for you today. The body of Mr. Gordon, the security attaché traveling with Lady Jane Brighton, was found dead by hanging at the lighthouse keeper's cottage this morning. We are unaware of the circumstances or any sinister motives. We will send word to the authorities on the mainland for police support. I have organized to send news this morning by way of a letter to the local ferry service that will be arriving soon at their scheduled stop. In the meantime, as per our usual protocol, we ask you to stay clear of the lighthouse until further notice. We are in the process of consoling Lady Jane on the loss of her dear and trusted long-time servant."

There was a mumble in the hall as villagers talked amongst themselves, expressing their shock at the news. It had been a long time since Solitary Island had suffered the death of a visitor from the mainland.

"Are there any questions?" The Elder sat back in his chair and calmly waited with his arms crossed over his chest. He uncontrollably fidgeted with his foot by tapping constantly. The townsfolk had become accustomed to it and barely noticed. They were unaware of his early onset of Parkinson's disease.

"It's Betwixt up to its old tricks again," called out one villager, an older man with a long black beard and shoulder-length hair. He spoke with a lisp and was known for speaking his mind.

The Elder shrugged his shoulders and crossed his legs as he anticipated the question every time there was a village announcement about a misfortune.

"Mr. Macnaught, I think it's premature to blame Betwixt, although I understand your point of view. I will be sending Dahlia Ravenscroft and Paranormal Jack to investigate and see if it has anything to do with this unfortunate event." He cleared his throat once more and took a deep breath.

"And what's the point calling for a police inspector from the mainland anyway. They don't know our culture and our ways. They will cause more anxiety rather than solve the problem." It was the old village women who had a distaste for anyone from the mainland.

"The last time the police arrived, they spent most of their time on the beach. They made up this story of searching the coastline for the body until Freddy caught them going for a dip in the nude!"

The townsfolk broke out into laughter, having become used to her banter.

"Yes, Ms Peggsworth. I understand your concern, and I agree. But we have no choice. They have authority over the islands. We are not separated from the mainland, where crime and the police are concerned. Let them do their work and take the body away. That part of it will be of service to us. And you know, they hate coming here, so it will be quick as usual. And by the way...I don't think they will go skinny dipping in this chilly weather unless they have gone completely mad."

"But what about the Grave Wind...it comes along after every suspicious death. Do we need to take precautions?" An older man called out from the back of the hall.

"Mr. Johnstone. That is true, and it's something we are keeping an eye on. We all know the early signs of the Grave Wind—a shift in wind patterns to the east, the stench of a rotting corpse, and the sudden drop in temperature. The birds disappear, and the animals start behaving erratically."

"Just like my wife, Maya, although she's like that all the time and doesn't need the Grave Wind to set her off!" said Mr. Maclean. He had a crooked smile and a missing front tooth.

His wife, Maya, slapped him on the shoulder while shaking her head. She knew what he was like, as it was not the first time he had tried to be funny at her expense.

Everyone in the room stood up and exited row by row, except for Dahlia and Paranormal Jack, who remained at the Elder's request to discuss the next steps. This is because investigating a death that could be associated with the paranormal followed an old village protocol, particularly if it were suspected Betwixt had something to do with it.

Dahlia and Paranormal Jack walked towards the Elder at a brisk pace and huddled next to him. They knew the drill and what was expected. The Elder would lay down the rules for investigating the paranormal events at the lighthouse keeper's cottage to ensure the correct process. And this meant avoiding engaging with Betwixt at any cost. To keep an open mind and not become manipulated by its shenanigans and cons.

"My dear paranormals…I couldn't say this while communicating with the town folk." He coughed slightly while placing his handkerchief over his mouth. "You know when you are getting too old, a nagging cough sticks around for longer than it should. I've been trying to fight this bug off for a while, and yes, my dear, your herbal remedies have helped bring it under control—at least, it's not getting worse."

Dahlia nodded and said, "Yes, the Saint John's Wort powder needs to be increased now that your cough is in the final stretch. To calm the nerves down."

"Hmm, I didn't think about that, my dear."

"Yes, stress can have a bearing on your recovery too."

"Well, with all this stuff that's going on with Lady Jane, I'm going to need it." He paused for a moment to reflect and placed his hands gently on Dahlia and Paranormal Jack's shoulders. "Yes, there is no question it's Betwixt," he said quietly. "I mean, who else could it have been. It has all the hallmarks of someone driven to suicide and just the way Betwixt likes it."

"We'll tread carefully and look for any signs," said Dahlia.

The Elder nodded. "Good, and don't engage Betwixt. It will know you're here. Probably did this to draw you in, but I'm being hypothetical—it's my gut feeling."

At the lighthouse keeper's cottage, where Lady Jane had spent her first night, she was awakened by the clamor of voices outside her room. The sun was beginning to peak over the horizon as its rays filtered through the cracks in the window frame. An unexpected flurry of people from Haven's End descended on the lighthouse at sunrise. And in keeping with the usual controversy surrounding Solitary Island, Lady Jane was about to find out the fate of her trusted aid, Mr. Gordon.

She thrust the sheets off her bed while her feet became entangled. She tugged even harder by kicking the sheets in frustration while reaching for her robe and slippers. She could feel the tension in the air and couldn't help foreseeing the worst was yet to come. She had endured a broken sleep and couldn't settle down in her unfamiliar environment. There was something in her room that kept her awake all night. A spiritual presence that she could sense. Lady Jane had concluded that she was not alone and that a poltergeist had engulfed the lighthouse and become a perilous lost spirit. She felt its torment, anger, and confusion all rolled up into a bucket of schizophrenic behavior.

Lady Jane tied her robe effortlessly and unlocked the bedroom door. She became frustrated as the old mortice lock required a jiggle to open the latch, all while her trademark impatience took the better of her.

She walked steadily to the main entrance of the lighthouse cottage to be greeted by Paranormal Jack and Dahlia.

"Lady Jane, good morning," said Paranormal Jack in a guarded tone while Dahlia acknowledged her with a nod.

"Something has happened, and it's not good news, isn't it?" Lady Jane prompted with an inquisitive look—her eyes wide.

Paranormal Jack shuffled his feet in the dirt. More of a nervous reaction until Dahlia decided to take charge of the communication.

"Mr. Gordon is dead." Dahlia realized she had to be straight up.

"He's dead? Did I hear you correctly, Dahlia?"

"Yes, Ma'am. The housekeeper found him this morning.

"But how did he die? This is a shock to me. He was my loyal aid for twenty years and a good friend of my father." Lady Jane placed her hands over weeping eyes and dropped her head."

"We are so sorry, Ma'am. It's come as a shock to the entire village." Dahlia continued to lead the conversation while Paranormal Jack looked on.

"How did it happen?"

"Hanging, Ma'am."

"He hanged himself in his room. But what on Earth drove him to that?"

"We don't know. We have notified the authorities on the mainland. They are coming on the next ship."

Lady Jane grabbed onto the shoulder of Paranormal Jack to maintain her balance as she was ready to faint. He instinctively stiffened his body to support her weight, acting as an anchor.

"He didn't have a worry in the world. He had no financial issues; he neither gambled nor drank. He had no family or problems with those close to him. Mr. Gordon was the most stable and reliable man one could imagine."

Dahlia placed her hand on her shoulder to console Lady Jane. "I understand the pain, Ma'am, and the distress this has brought on you. If there is anything we can do to support you, please…we are here for you."

Lady Jane took a handkerchief from her pocket and wiped her tears. She paused for a while as she came to terms with the situation and then blew her nose.

"Have you pulled down the body from the noose?"

"Yes, Ma'am. He's been placed on the floor while we wait for the coroner to arrive. As you would understand, we are not allowed to touch anything until then."

"Can I see his body?"

Dahlia and Paranormal Jack looked at each other, unsure how to respond.

"We will check with our village Elder. He's just over there at the entrance to the lighthouse. He's going to check Mr. Gordon's quarters to ensure everything is in place for the investigators."

Lady Jane was renowned for having a mind of her own, and her upper-class pompous attitude was not going to settle with that response. She lifted her head, pursed her lips, and headed to the Elder, stomping her feet with every step, disregarding established protocols. Nobody was going to tell her what to do. She walked to the lighthouse entrance in a determined manner, leaving Dahlia and Paranormal Jack behind.

Paranormal Jack turned to Dahlia. "Should we call her back?"

Dahlia shrugged her shoulders. "I don't think she is the type to take instructions from anyone. And besides, we are not the police, and it's not our job to control Lady Jane."

Paranormal Jack agreed. "We came here to pass on the bad news to her just like the Elder instructed. As for all the other stuff, she will need to take it up with him."

Paranormal Jack sat on the fallen log beside them, crossing his feet and folding his arms. Dahlia could sense that something was on his mind.

"Come on. Say it, Jack…"

He smiled in advance before unleashing his point of view. "It was Betwixt. Right?"

"Of course, that's what the Elder believes, and he has been around a lot longer than us. But, we can't say that to Lady Jane."

"That sneaky shapeshifter must have had something on Mr. Gordon to push him to suicide. I wonder what it could be?" Paranormal Jack blinked his eyes.

Dahlia threw her hands up in the air. "Well, Jack, perhaps he was not as squeaky clean as Lady Jane made him out to be. A chink in his armor, so to speak."

"He may have a sinister past or a dark side. Who knows…" Paranormal Jack struggled to find the right words, but Dahlia knew what he meant.

"That's how Betwixt operates. It forces you to confront your past demons and holds you to account." Dahlia looked him straight in the eye. "It's how it sustains its evil appetite."

"Like a vampire and blood…" Paranormal Jack snuffed by blowing out a deep breath.

In front of the lighthouse entrance, an animated Lady Jane could be seen arguing with the Elder, demanding to be allowed to view Mr. Gordon's body. He was a feeble older man on a walking stick and barely had the strength to hold her back. Unlike the towns on the mainland, Haven's End had no police, as was prohibited in the town's charter. A kind of utopian existence where everyone loved everyone else and lived in harmony.

"I think we'd better help the Elder," suggested Dahlia in a lighthearted manner.

Paranormal Jack tried to downplay the situation by seeing the funny side and agreed to help.

"Lady Jane," she called out, waving to grab her attention.

She threw up her hands in frustration and took a deep breath.

"This man won't let me see Mr. Gordon's body, and I demand it!" She pointed to the lighthouse entrance. "I have a right to identify his body, at least."

Dahlia glanced towards the Elder and sought to give him assurances.

"How about Paranormal Jack and I accompany Lady Jane to view the body without touching anything?"

The Elder paused for a moment and then nodded reluctantly. "Make it quick because I'm the one who must deal with the authorities and not you. It shouldn't take long to identify a body. A couple minutes only…"

They all turned to each other, waiting for someone to take the lead. Dahlia took on the responsibility of leading Lady Jane to the door.

"Follow me, Ma'am," she said.

"I'll come too." Paranormal Jack did not want to be left behind with the Elder.

As they made their way to the lighthouse entrance, Lady Jane stopped in her tracks and took hold of Dahlia's arm.

"Young lady, I had the strangest encounter last night," Lady Jane turned to Dahlia with a curious look.

"Oh, and what was it, Ma'am?"

"It was late at night and dark, with only the light from a candle on the side table. I heard a moan, but not just any cry for help—it was shrouded in pain. I felt the agony of this poltergeist."

Paranormal Jack was curious and the first to ask about it. "And what did you see, Ma'am"

"A young lady—a very pretty one with long flowing hazelnut colored hair and a beautiful white lace dress.

She had the perfect smile and waved me to come forward until it all changed in an instant. She pranced around at first, tip-toing about like a ballerina until she stopped unexpectedly and growled like a hyena. It was ear-piercing and went right through your skin. It gave me chills, and I shriveled."

"Oh, tell us more, Ma'am. We have heard stories about the ghost of Lydia Gow haunting this lighthouse."

"Has a bathtub got anything to do with it?"

"You saw her coming out of the bathtub?" Paranormal Jack's line of questioning was straight to the point."

Lady Jane placed the palm of her hand on the wall and closed her eyes. "I felt her energy just like I'm doing now. I felt her pain, and she was reaching out for help. A deep-seated agony like no other I have ever encountered." She dropped her hands as though they had become unstuck and opened her eyes, frowning and pursing her lips. "Yes, she was in a bathtub waving her arms about and screaming for help—the desperate pleas of a young girl who had just found out she was dead."

Dahlia and Paranormal Jack stood silent as they absorbed the vivid description from Lady Jane.

"Before we inspect the body of Mr. Gordon, perhaps I should explain the story of Lydia Gow," said Dahlia.

"Oh yes, my dear, tell me."

"Lydia Gow fell ill in November 1912, and her father, the principal lighthouse keeper, called for a doctor from the mainland. Heavy seas and fierce winds hampered the doctor's journey. When he arrived, it was too late."

"Oh, what a tragic situation for any parent," commented Lady Jane.

"Lydia had contracted typhoid, and in those days, it was basically fatal. She passed away before they could get her off the island. With the storm raging, there was no way of getting Lydia's body to the mainland for days, and burial was not an option. The island is nearly all rock, and there was no topsoil that they could dig up to make a temporary grave."

"No, don't tell me they buried her in the…"

"Yes, Ma'am, in the bathtub. Her mother did not want her body thrown into the sea, so she was placed inside one of two bathtubs, covered in concrete and lime, before the tubs were soldered together. The teenager was buried on the mainland four days after her death, and according to sources, they thought she was still alive inside the tub...or they could hear the screams occasionally.

"Did Lydia really leave the island? Her soul is still here in this very place. Isn't it." Lady Jane said confidently.

"If you speak to the Elders, they will tell you that her spirit remains on Solitary Island, caught in what we call the *in-between*," Dahlia confirmed the tale. "A place where you're dead but have not moved on to the other side. Caught in a horrible place that brings nothing but terror to your soul. An endless pit of nothingness, sadness, and evil combined. You can't get out, or at least you don't know how to find a way. That's why we call it the *in-between*.

Lady Jane realized that Dahlia's explanation of the *in-between* was beyond a description; it was a personal one.

"You've been there, haven't you?" Lady Jane nodded as she caressed Dahlia's face with both hands. "I feel your pain, my dear."

Dahlia nodded but couldn't say a word. She held her breath and then exhaled in short spasms as she clenched her fist. Blinking rapidly while pressing on her lips, her eyes twitched.

"Oh, I didn't mean to cause your memories to

engulf you. It was to tell you that they could have been lucid dreams. Did you ever think about that possibility?"

Paranormal Jack turned towards Lady Jane while raising his eyebrows. "What is a lucid dream?"

"A lucid dream can occur when the sleeper is aware that they are in a dream and can exercise control over their environment. During a lucid dream, you're aware that the events are not real, even though the dream feels vivid and real. You may be able to control how the action unfolds. You might be doing something active inside your dream, such as flying, for example."

"You can actually do that?' Paranormal Jack was stoked by the thought.

Lady Jane smiled and placed her hand on his arm. "Oh, and you don't need to worry. A spiritual connection is necessary for individuals to experience that attachment in their dreams. She paused to take a breath and continued. "A lucid dream is a type of dream wherein the dreamer realizes that they are dreaming. But you could be trained because it is a skill that can be attained—with the right teacher, of course."

"Oh, I would like that Lady Brighton…very much so."

They paused for a moment of reflection and gathered their thoughts.

"Let's see the body of Mr. Gordon," said Dahlia.

Lady Jane nodded without saying a word, following her through the lighthouse entrance. She was reluctant to see the body of her trusted aid but knew it had to be done for her own peace of mind.

7

SILENT REEF

A jagged, mist-cloaked expanse of coral and shattered rock, Silent Reef lies on the fringes of the known seas at the northern tip of Solitary Island.

In this treacherous labyrinth, the ocean itself whispers secrets. The reef is named for the eerie hush that blankets it; even the wind and waves seem subdued as if the place itself forbids noise.

By day, the waters shimmer with an unnatural opalescence, casting a ghostly glow on the craggy coral formations that rise like skeletal fingers from the depths. But at night, the reef transforms—phosphorescent lights pulse beneath the waves, illuminating shadowy figures that move just out of sight. Some say these are bioluminescent fish, while others claim they are the spirits of drowned sailors, forever bound to the currents as their cries for help go unanswered.

Despite its morbid reputation, Silent Reef is a place of hidden wonders. Ancient ruins, half-submerged and worn smooth by time, hint at a lost Indigenous tribe that once called this place home. Divers have reported glimpses of strange glyphs carved into the coral, their meanings lost to the ages. On a cloudless day, you see the tips of wooden hulls that crashed into the reefs during tempestuous storms, taking innocent souls.

Few dare to venture here willingly. Superstitious sailors whisper of ghost ships that vanish into the mist, never to be seen again and of haunting melodies carried on the wind—songs that lure the unsuspecting into the reef's embrace, where jagged rocks and unseen predators await. Yet, for those who seek lost relics, forbidden knowledge, or hidden pathways through the sea, Silent Reef is both a peril and a promise.

The most terrifying tale of Silent Reef is the cursed song. On certain nights, when the moon is a thin sliver in the sky, a melody drifts across the water—low, mournful, yet irresistible. Those who hear it feel an overwhelming urge to follow, stepping off their ships as if sleepwalking, vanishing into the mist. Some had been found later, floating lifelessly in the water, their eyes wide open, faces frozen in expressions of rapture or terror. Others were never found at all.

Some think the song is summoning victims. In contrast, others believe it is the last remnant of those already lost souls bound to the reef, endlessly repeating their sorrowful lament.

Despite its dangers, Silent Reef remains a place of grim fascination. Some believe that within its depths, relics of the lost tribe still hold power—artifacts that might grant knowledge of the Silent Maw or even the means to control it. There are whispers of a forgotten temple submerged beneath the waves, where priests once prayed to keep the entity at bay…or to wake it.

Few dare to seek such knowledge, but for those who do, the reef offers both peril and promise. For those who linger too long, however, one truth remains: no one leaves Silent Reef unchanged.

Poking out of the hill directly behind the swollen cliffs is the cave of Forsaken Rock. Long ago, Forsaken Rock was said to be a place of ritual—a temple, a prison, or both. Legends speak of an ancient being, neither mortal nor God, bound within its walls. Whether it was once human or something far older, none can say. Still, the curse it left behind remains— the Grave Wind that blankets the island and town of

Haven's End repeatedly.

The deeper one ventures into Forsaken Rock, the more reality itself begins to unravel. Shadows move where there should be none. Walls shift when no one is looking. Whispers rise from the dark, speaking in voices eerily familiar—sometimes taking the form of lost loved ones, sometimes one's own voice calling back.

But the true horror of Forsaken Rock lies in its heart—a great, yawning chasm said to hold the Forsaken Maw, a void that consumes all light, all sound, all hope. The deeper one gazes into it, the more it gazes back. Those who stare too long are said to lose themselves—not their bodies, but something deeper, something irreplaceable.

Some return with no memory of who they were. Others leave with a new voice speaking from their throats, their eyes dark with something that was not there before. But most are never seen again.

The entity bound within Forsaken Rock is not dead, only dreaming. It feeds on the minds of those who enter, growing stronger with each lost soul. Some say it was a god cast down for its crimes, others that it was once a mortal who sought forbidden knowledge and was consumed by the very power they wished to control.

What is known is this—Forsaken Rock does not let go of those it takes. There are stories of people disappearing into the cave, only to be seen again years later, unchanged by time, their faces twisted into hollow imitations of life. They do not speak. They do not blink. And when they vanish once more, they leave no trace behind.

Some whisper that the cave is not just a prison but a mouth—that each lost soul is a sacrifice, feeding the thing within, bringing it closer to waking. And when it does, the world itself may tremble.

As for the Villagers, it was prohibited. Nobody within Haven's End really knew why— it was a law to be obeyed - handed down by the Elders.

Despite its terrifying reputation, Forsaken Rock draws those who seek power, answers, or redemption. Scholars, occultists, and desperate souls have all risked their minds and lives to uncover its secrets. Some claim that deep within the cave lies an artifact of immeasurable power, a key to controlling the darkness or releasing it. Others believe that the curse can be broken, but only if one is willing to make an unthinkable sacrifice.

No one knows the truth, for truth itself is a fragile

thing within Forsaken Rock. Memories twist, time fractures and reality bends—but the cave remains, waiting, always waiting. And somewhere in the dark, something listens.

Truth be known, that was Lady Jane's hidden agenda—to get to Forsaken Rock and explore the evil that resided within. According to her studies, she believed it was where the island's curse of the Grave Wind originated from. The center of evil and the shroud of death. Something happened there when the first settlers arrived, stumbling upon the ancient curse and unleashing it without realizing its potency.

But it was going to be challenging to get to Silent Reef without her trusted attaché. Lady Jane had to draw on Dahlia's and Paranormal Jack's curiosity and rebellious spirits by bending the long-standing rules of the Elders. This represented a problem—find a way to Silent Reef or leave Solitary Island and abandon her mission empty-handed.

Dahlia and Paranormal Jack stood quietly at the pier, watching the supply ship anchor. Mr. Gordon's body was wrapped in a white sheet, waiting to be loaded onto the ship. There was no undertaker or morgue on Solitary Island, and they had to make do with what they had. Fortunately, the captain of the vessel had been accompanied by a police inspector from the mainland who brought a body bag to prepare it for transport.

Lady Jane stood by the body of her trusted confidant, meticulously making sure that the transfer process onto the ship was compassionate and smooth. Holding a long white handkerchief over her eyes, she pretended it was to protect her face from the sea breeze—but everyone could sense she was wiping her tears. Not a lady of emotion and a tough one at that, her gentler side was on show for all to see. And while the chain tugged on the steel frame that held Mr. Gordon's body and commenced raising it into the air, she knew that was it, and he would be gone forever. She reached out to touch his body one more time, caressing him on the head for the very last time.

"Goodbye, Mr. Gordon. God bless you." A tear rolled down her cheek.

She turned toward Dahlia and Paranormal Jack and waved for a moment before a member of the ship's crew took her bag and escorted her to the gangway and onto the boat.

"She's leaving?" said Paranormal Jack.

"I'm as surprised as you are. I thought she was going

to take us to the other side of the island."

"To Silent Reef…"

"Yes, Jack. The place that's forbidden."

"I was prepared to break the rule, you know."

Dahlia smiled and clasped her hands. "I wouldn't expect anything less from you."

Dahlia and Paranormal Jack waved a courteous goodbye to Lady Jane as she stepped onto the ship.

"I will miss her, you know Jack. She was different from anyone I have met before."

Paranormal Jack raised his shoulders like he always did when he had something to say.

"What is it, Jack?"

He puffed and pointed to the cliffs and beyond. "I had a feeling she knew something about this place. More than she was letting on."

"Umm, so did I, and I was hoping to get it out of her during our next conversation. But that won't be happening anytime soon."

"She mentioned Forsaken Rock for someone who claimed to have never been there before, let alone explored the island."

Dahlia nodded. "Yeah, I found that strange also. I would say ninety-nine percent of tourists who come here don't have a clue about Forsaken Rock and the cursed cave the Elders talk about. And yet she spoke about it with such confidence, it was as though she was remarkably familiar."

The ship roared its engine as the large bulk frame pulled away from the jetty into the open water. The smell of diesel from the ship's engine blew over the village. And in a pristine environment like Solitary Island, it was a smell that hung in the air.

Paranormal Jack placed his hand over his mouth and nose and cringed. "I will never get used to that smell."

In the meantime, their focus had moved to the police inspector. He was an unassuming man with a three-day beard, scruffy brown hair, and a slightly overweight pot. He appeared untidy from a distance, with his shirt hanging out from his trousers and a woolen pullover that had seen better days. Never mind the small holes that looked like moths had gotten to it. He constantly lifted his pants as they struggled to grip around his belly fat—tightening his belt continually, only for it to slip underneath his stomach again. It wasn't his first trip to Solitary Island, and the ship's crew identified with him as they jumped to his beck and call—*yes sir and no sir* was the common phrase.

The Elder had asked Dahlia to greet the police

inspector at the jetty and take him to the lighthouse cottage where Mr. Gordon had hanged himself. Despite his death being fresh on everyone's mind, the Elders wanted him to get straight to work, complete his investigation, and leave. The sooner this tragic incident was over, the sooner the people of Haven's End could get on with their lives.

The Elder knew the first action the police inspector would take would be to treat the lighthouse cottage as a crime scene and undertake a preliminary assessment. He would come by prepared with police tape to cordon off the area and a snappy camera hanging around his neck to take evidentiary photos for his report. With a notebook tucked away in his side pocket, he looked like he was all the part of a sleuth.

The police inspector was pointed in the direction of Dahlia and Paranormal Jack, who were waiting. He picked up his overnight bag and walked towards them at a slow pace. He had a noticeable slight limp on his right leg that wobbled each time his foot landed on the ground. And his body language contained a sense of displeasure—because police inspectors disliked visiting the island. They just wanted to do what was required and get out on the next ship.

Greeting them both with a bent smile and a solid

handshake, he grunted and cleared his throat. The smell of tobacco combined with coffee filled the air as he exhaled, dropping his bag to the ground with a thump.

"So, the Elder sent a bunch of kids to greet me this time." He looked at them both with an intense stare.

Dahlia didn't respond as she wanted to demonstrate her maturity and poise.

"We've been sent by the Elder to take you to the crime scene, and of course, if you're staying overnight, we have a room for you in town."

"Nice to meet you both. I'm Inspector Wellock." He then pointed to the lighthouse, " That is the room I stayed last time. I can't use it tonight?"

"It's the same room Mr. Gordon died, so we didn't think it would be appropriate, sir." Dahlia was quick with her response.

"Yes, that makes sense. And the village is fine then. Just make sure it's not next to that smelly piggery." He turned towards the ship's captain and waved goodbye as was often the custom to bid him a bon voyage. The police inspector then turned to Dahlia while rubbing his hands.

"Can you tell me how he died?"

"Suicide, I mean hanging…" Paranormal Jack

couldn't wait to join the conversation."

"And who are you, my dear boy?"

"Everyone calls me Paranormal Jack."

"Oh, so you're the mystique one? And what makes you paranormal? Special powers? Ha, ha."

Dahlia interrupted the police inspector's sarcasm by attempting to bring him back on track with the conversation.

"Sir, it was death by hanging and suicide, definitely."

"I see, the man killed himself then. Well, that's going to be a quick investigation. No foul play and just a man who went crazy." He paused and looked around the island beyond the jetty and the sharp cliffs that lined the shore. "You know this place is renowned for suicides. I've been investigating them for over twenty years—the same story repeatedly. Tourists, death, and suicide."

Dahlia and Paranormal Jack were taken aback by the police inspector's quick wit.

"Well, I've done my homework on Mr. Gordon, and the ship's log states he had been here before—on his own. The captain certainly remembers him."

"Oh, he remembers all his passengers?" said Dahlia.

"Yes, the uncommon ones, that's for sure. Mr.

Gordon was always impeccably dressed and carried a gun with him—well known amongst the ship's crew. Then, he would change into mountain gear before disembarking. He would ask the ship's captain to place his belongings into the cabin for the return journey the next day."

There was dead silence, with only the roar of the ship's engine in the background as it chugged away from the jetty.

"So, you're going to ask me what he was doing here, I assume?" The police inspector blinked and nodded his head.

"Yes, we're very curious because nobody in Haven's End noticed his presence in the past.

The police inspector laughed. "With all due respect, miss, I don't think anyone in this town would pay too much attention to anything unless it's a storm brewing—a Grave Wind perhaps."

He knows about it, she thought.

"He went to Forsaken Rock—you know that place? It's forbidden, right?"

"Yes, next to Silent Reef." Paranormal Jack interjected. "Our Elders tell us it's a cursed place, and everyone who goes there comes out a different person as though their whole personality was…"

"…kidnapped right? Like an evil possession of sorts." The police inspector calmly picked up his bag and turned in the direction of the lighthouse. "Well, let's go and check out this room then. I want to wrap up this investigation today and get the next ship out tomorrow."

Dahlia led the way, followed by the stooping police inspector and Paranormal Jack. As they reached the main gate to the lighthouse, an eerie feeling went through her bones, and she shook her shoulders. It was an instinctive reaction, as though someone had poked a small needle into their skin.

"Are you alright, miss?" asked the police inspector.

"It's waiting for us,"

"What is waiting for us…can you be more specific? And please don't say it's a spirit or a ghost."

"The same thing that killed Mr. Gordon, Oh, and don't think pulling out your gun will make a difference—it's not from this world." Dahlia was not holding back.

"A ghost, my dear? A creature from the beyond? The spirit world awaits me. Ha. Ha. I have heard it all before. There's nothing there, but small-town superstition drummed into your head from an early age by those village Elders. Can't you see how you've been conditioned by those quacks with long white beards?"

He thrust the door open and pointed to a room. "If I recall from my last visit, this is the guest quarters."

Dahlia nodded without saying a word.

The police inspector looked around the room, struggling against the minimal filtered light from the small window. He dropped his bag and quickly unzipped the inside pocket—pulling out a small hand torch. Holding it in a pencil grip, he directed the light to where the suicide occurred.

"Hmm, so that's where he hanged himself." He stepped forward, reaching out for the noose. "I couldn't have tied a better knot myself. Looks like he'd had a lot of practice to get it that perfect."

"You don't think it was his first attempt?" said Paranormal Jack.

"Nah, not unless he was working as an executioner. This noose has craftmanship written all over it." The police inspector smiled back at Paranormal Jack, but it could have been construed as a cheeky grin.

"And that must be the flimsy chair he kicked himself off the ground. Yeah, I'm surprised it could hold his body weight without collapsing."

The police inspector pointed to broken glass on the floor next to the chair. "It was the bottle of grog that must have fallen out of his hands. It looks like his first attempt failed."

There was a sudden, unnatural and biting breeze swept through the room. The door behind slammed shut with a force that sent a tremor through the floor. Dahlia's breath itched. The temperature plummeted in an instant; the warmth of the room was swallowed by an unnatural chill that burrowed deep into her bones. She could see her breath now, curling in front of her like ghostly fingers.

Then came the smell. A rancid, putrid stench of decay thickened the air, coating her tongue with the sickly taste of rot. It was the smell of something long dead, of flesh turned rancid. Dahlia gagged, clamping a hand over her mouth, but the stench forced its way into her lungs, suffocating, inescapable.

A metallic clatter echoed against the wall. The small ship's anchor fixed securely began to rattle. It trembled violently as though unseen hands gripped it, desperate to rip it free. The sound of grinding metal scraped against her nerves, growing louder and more frenzied until it threatened to shatter completely.

Dahlia's pulse pounded in her ears. She could feel it—whatever it was, it was here.

Something unseen loomed in the shadows, pressing

against the edges of reality, just beyond the reach of her vision. The air felt thick, suffocating, as though something enormous filled the room, twisting the space around it. The walls seemed to close in, warping like melted wax, the shadows stretching unnaturally.

A whisper slithered through the dark. Not words, not entirely. A rasping, guttural sound, low and curling around the edges of her sanity, seeping into her mind, fingers pressing against her skull. It carried the weight of something ancient, something that had lingered long before she had ever stepped into this place.

She tried to move, but her body refused. Her limbs felt weighed down, held fast by an unseen force. Her breath came in shallow gasps, her heart hammering against her ribs. Something watched her, not with eyes, but with a presence that curled around her like a noose.

Then, from the corner of her eye, she saw it.

A shadow darker than the rest. Twisting, moving, and reaching.

Dahlia's scream caught in her throat as the anchor finally broke free from the wall with a deafening crack and hurtled toward her. And then it shifted.

Before her, the darkness convulsed, its form bubbling and splitting like flesh stretched too thin. It twisted and reshaped itself, one moment tall and gaunt, the next hunched and crawling, flickering between forms as if cycling through stolen identities. Its mouth, if it could be called that, gaped open in a silent scream, jagged teeth shifting with each new grotesque shape it took.

Dahlia's stomach churned as it settled into something disturbingly familiar—her own reflection, but wrong. The eyes were hollow pits, the mouth curling into a grin far too broad, skin sagging as though barely clinging to the bones beneath. It stepped forward, mimicking her movements with an eerie precision.

A distorted voice rasped from its shifting throat, a cruel echo of her own, "You let me in. Now, I wear your skin."

The glass frame picture of the first lighthouse keeper broke free from the wall with a deafening crack and hurtled toward her as the poltergeist lunged.

The police inspector reacted by instinctively taking hold of Dahlia's hand and pulling her down as the picture frame wisped past and splitting a hair.

"It's Betwixt!" Dahlia called out in a state of panic.

"It's been a long time since you were in my grip." Betwixt slithered with a fork tongue by altering its shape. "But you have someone with you today—an inspector from the mainland who couldn't give a dam about the suicide. He just wanted a day out of the office. Oh, he didn't say that all the inspectors thought it was so funny that they elected to pick straws. To see who would get the day out."

Betwixt curled its tongue around its lips as it exhaled a green spit all over the police inspector's face.

"And as for Mr. Gordon…well, he is with me now roaming around in the *in-between*. Running amok like a cry-baby and blaming everyone for his death. But I didn't ask him to kill himself, and he shouldn't have gone to Forsaken Rock in the first place. That's where the damage was done. They played with his mind, making him feel depressed and useless. Asking him to do things that were against his moral values."

The police inspector pulled out a handkerchief from his trouser pocket and wiped his face in disgust— pointing directly to Betwixt. His face creased with rage from the insult lashed at him.

Betwixt laughed aloud, filling the room with a high-pitched echo. "Oh, and what are you going to do now. Pull out your gun and shoot me. I'm transparent, and I can change shape, and best of all, I can disappear in front of your eyes in an instant and watch the bullet go right through me from across the room. I am eternal and can live forever—and while that is a blessing and curse at the same time—I'm only half dead. One foot in your world and one foot in mine." Betwixt slithered and morphed into a little girl in a white dress, curly hair tied on a ribbon and dressed as though in a pantomime. To say she had an angelic face was an understatement—this little girl was so pretty she oozed splendor amongst the mere mortals.

Dahlia stood up and pointed to Betwixt. "Well, I know your attention-seeking habits are on display. Great! You've made your point, but I know you need something, or you wouldn't have shown up. It must be worth your time. Right?"

"Oh, my dear, your sharp wit is all I need today to feed my ego. And yes, I have a task for you. The same task that I provided to Mr. Gordon failed miserably. And look what happened to him." Betwixt positioned itself underneath the noose and tied it around its next, poking its tongue. It then kicked off the chair— dangling its feet while mimicking suffocation while its face turned red.

"Did you like that? It was fun watching Mr. Gordon hang himself and die…" Betwixt slithered again with greater intensity. "I have a proposition for you." Betwixt laughed loudly again but with a twist of a childish giggle.

"I won't make a deal with you, Betwixt, and succumb to your poison chalice. You're like a Venus fly trap trying to catch me off guard. And then you use your wit to convince me it's the right thing to do."

Betwixt danced about lifting its toes like an Irish ballet dancer—tiptoeing across the room while raising its arms in the air in an arch type of movement.

"It's fine. It just means I need to coerce you."

The police inspector uncontrollably lifted from the ground as an invisible force took grip of him. He elevated six inches from the tip of his toes and was carried directly underneath the noose. The police inspector kicked and threw his arms about in a savage exhibition of a fight back, but it made no difference. The noose wiggled into position over his neck as it tightened.

"My dear, you either do as I ask and carry out my proposition, or you can watch the police inspector die in front of your eyes. I'll hang him by the neck and watch his face turn red while his eyes bug outwards like marbles. And I can make it as gruesome as I like. I will make his eyes pop out or his teeth bite off his own lips. Surely this must bring memories from ten years ago when we went through a similar proposition?"

The police inspector called out to stop as fear gripped him. Even though death had surrounded him in his role all his working life, he wasn't prepared for his premature death in these circumstances."

"Stop it! Stop it!" screamed the police inspector as he clung to life. The noose was firmly around his neck, and by now, it continued to tighten, causing him to cough violently. Betwixt kicked the chair underneath his legs to make way for the last step.

"If you observe, my dear, this is the part I like most when they are no longer aware of their senses as the body begins to shut down. Do you like it? Can you feel it? The energy of death in front of your eyes. And if you wait a little longer, there's the crescendo."

"Fine, let him go, and I will do what you ask—don't kill him!" Dahlia threw her fist in the air in a defiant move, although it made no difference to the outcome. She had just made the biggest mistake one could with Betwixt. She was compromised to a devilish task, and unless she executed it according to the demands of Betwixt, she would suffer the same fate as Mr. Gordon.

The police inspector dropped to the ground semiconscious while holding his neck.

"I am alive?" He looked towards Dahlia for confirmation while gasping for air. "Yes. Yes, I am?"

Dahlia nodded but without showing any emotion. She had just made a deal with the devil to save someone she didn't know, and probably no one in the village cared about. Had she taken a significant risk? The likes she could go on to regret. And yet, something underpinning her faith made her do it. She had reconnected with Betwixt, not because she wanted to but because it could unlock the secrets of the curse of Solitary Island and Forsaken Rock. It was a way in, although a dangerous path that put her in the firing line. There was no question about it. Her life was at risk unless she followed through on Betwixt's demands.

"I knew you would come to your senses," said Betwixt. It changed its shape from a little girl to a dancing mannequin with a distorted body and an oversized head. To say it was gruesome was an understatement. It was, for all intents, a monster.

Dahlia and Paranormal Jack dashed towards the police inspector as he coughed and spat phlegm while regaining his breath. His pale face and rolled eyes showed how close he had come to death. They had saved him just in time.

"Here is the deal, my dear. You will go to Forsaken Rock with a pickaxe. When you arrive, you will enter the cave at the very top of the cliff—do you know where it is? You've been there before and never told anyone. You broke the rules of the Elders as you normally do."

Paranormal Jack turned to Dahlia instinctively and said while shaking his head. "You've been there before? And you never told me?"

"Yes, Jack, a couple of years ago, I went there on a hunch with a burning curiosity. Something pulled me there, and it was after the Grave Wind ravaged the town."

Betwixt was in no mood for conversation and wanted to get to the point—becoming impatient with fessing up.

"Who cares whether you've been there before. You're not the only one who has broken the Elders' rules. The whole bloody town has. You're all perfect at keeping things to yourselves." Betwixt scoffed at Dahia's admittance of guilt. "When you arrive at Forsaken Rock and enter the cave, you will find the stone carved out by Elijah Crane." And we won't talk about him too much as he was a crazy man who nearly destroyed the colony because of his fanatical cult beliefs."

"And what do you want me to do with this rock?" Dahlia responded angrily. Raising her voice to remonstrate her displeasure.

Betwixt lifted about one foot off the ground and twisted its head full circle while its neck cracked. "Ahh, that feels better." Repeating the movement one more time.

"Well, tell me. What is it I must do…"

"With your pickaxe, I want you to split the stone. And don't worry, it's not a large rock, the size of a large quern used to grind grain. A couple of sharp intrusions into the middle should do it. It's over a hundred years old and worn down over time."

"Is that it? Just smash a stone."

Betwixt paused. "Well, it might fight back. I mean, try to hurt you?"

"A stone that will try to hurt me. It's not a living thing."

"Oh, my dear." Betwixt sighed, exhaling a large amount of air toward Dahlia and Paranormal Jack, which smelled like rotting meat. "How little you know about the powers of Forsaken Rock, the curse of Solitary Island, and where the Grave Wind was born. This rock is bound by the energy of *Itzam-K'aa*. Who do you think put me here in the first place.?"

Dahlia crossed her arms defiantly and cringed. "You want me to break the curse and risk my life so you can be freed."

"Oh, don't get so emotional. If you don't like the idea and have second thoughts, I would gladly snap the police inspector's neck right now. Finish off the hanging while he is on the ground. Now that would be a sight…never killed someone like that before." Betwixt slithered its tongue and pranced about like a small child unable to control its joy.

Dahlia nodded reluctantly. "Fine, that's what you want. But let me remind you that you and I are not done yet. I will come back for you."

Within an instant, Betwixt disappeared, and with it, all the trappings of evil—the smell, the chill, and the feeling of being under a spell. For all intents, it was as though nothing happened. But make no mistake, Dahlia's challenge was real, and her life was at stake. She had accepted an undertaking that nobody had been able to achieve before. The odds were against her success, and the gravity of her situation was dire.

"I hope you're happy," said Paranormal Jack as he peered into the eyes of the police inspector. "She's put her life at risk for you."

8

FORSAKEN ROCK

They called it *Forsaken Rock long before* anyone dared to settle near it.

A jagged monolith of black granite jutting out from the forest floor like the broken fang of a buried god. The trees grew twisted around it; their trunks contorted as if recoiling from whatever pulsed beneath the stone. Birds never perched on it. Even the wind was hushed when it passed. But the settlers came anyway because it's human nature to be curious.

In the autumn of 1823, a dozen families laid claim to the rock, their ambitions outweighing their caution. And not for reasons that you would typically associate with a new colony. They didn't clear trees, build homes, or carve a church from the same grey timber that lined the hills. But one man—Elijah Crane—

broke the pact of silence. He split a stone from Forsaken Rock to build his foundation. He said it was a rock. Just earth. But something more sinister was taking place.

Three months later, he vanished. Every trace of him—gone. Not a drop of blood, not a single cry heard through the pines. Only the foundation remained, still warm to the touch, and black moss grew in the cracks. By winter's end, half the valley had fallen to madness: whispering voices in the night, animals flayed with surgical precision, children drawing symbols in the dirt they swore they'd never seen before. And it all started with a wind, and not just any type of tempest—this was different. It was the Grave Wind.

No one speaks of the original settlers now. And Forsaken Rock is banned by the Elders, save for the crows and the cold. And the rock—Forsaken still, but never silent. Still embedded in the psyche of the people of Haven's End.

They say if you stand too close to the stone carved by Elijah Crane when the sun bleeds down the ridge, you can hear it breathe.

What lies within Forsaken Rock is not merely a presence but a consciousness. Not a spirit in the traditional sense, nor a demon of any known folklore—

but something older. Something pre-human. Long before settlers crossed the ridge, before the land had a name, the tribes who roamed Solitary Island marked the place as taboo. Not out of superstition but remembrance. They spoke of Itzam-K'aa, "the hunger that waits beneath." Not a god. Not a devil. A buried intellect. Sentient energy, trapped in the rock like a wound in the earth's memory—sealed, not by chance, but by desperate ritual over a thousand years ago.

Geologists in modern times would call it an anomaly—a radiation signature beneath the stone, pulsing like a heartbeat, disrupting compasses and radio waves. But it's no natural phenomenon. And the Grave Wind is a manifestation of its powers—some say its anger—a tantrum like a volcano erupting spewing lava and ash.

The rock is a vessel. A prison built not of stone but binding. When Elijah Crane chiseled into it, he cracked more than granite. He unsealed a thread and an ominous power.

What lives inside is not made of flesh, yet it craves flesh to speak, to move, to be. It is an intelligence composed of will without form, like a virus of thought. An anti-consciousness invades the mind, eroding memory and replacing it with whispers. It doesn't possess people in the way myths suggest. That would be too basic, as would the stuff of demons. It unwrites them. Leaves their bodies to function as vessels—eyes that do not blink, mouths that smile without breath.

Over time, the rock feeds. Not on blood but belief. The more fear surrounds it, the stronger its reach. The children carve the symbols unknowingly. Those are its language. The dreams settlers shared of black oceans and burning skies? Those are its memories. Forsaken Rock is not haunted. It is awake.

There is the story of the one that got away and became its nemesis—Betwixt. Now, they had become mortal enemies, with Betwixt taking over one side of the island. In fact, they had split their territory in two. But it did not end well for Betwixt being cast into a world that is neither heaven nor hell but rather a constant misery—the *in-between*. And even though Betwixt was the one that got away, it had become cursed for eternity, trapped in non-existence, praying for those vulnerable victims to fill its void and hunger for depravity.

The only way out of its cursed life was to destroy the rock and the foundation that set the curse that had engulfed the island. Freeing itself would also remove the phenomena of the Grave Wind. In all the intertwining and connections that drove the curse and the pursuing evil, at the heart of it all was Forsaken Rock. These natural phenomena have become an ecological evil.

Dahlia and Paranormal Jack returned to Haven's End in search of the Elder. The police inspector who had been rattled by the experience with Betwixt only had one thing in mind—to return to the mainland. He wasn't interested in Dahlia's plight and that her life was at risk from Betwixt.

"He's usually at the poultry farm at this time of day," said Paranormal Jack.

Elders had become entrepreneurs supplying fresh food to the mainland. Leveraging with distributors, their products had loyal customers who sought a healthier alternative. In recent times, they have struggled to meet demand and haven't been able to grow their cooperative on an island limited to expansion. The Elders had discovered they could make more profit, making less, so it suited them to the ground.

Dahlia nodded and said, "Oh yes, and what a money spinner this has become. He's an accomplished egg farmer and could always be found at the poultry farm or loading the eggs on the jetty."

"Counting the dollars, hey."

"Yes, Jack, we've all seen him flash the roll of one hundred bills."

"And they are always bulging from his pocket." Paranormal Jack couldn't help but laugh as they often made fun of the Elder in a type of contradiction that beset Haven's End. The Elders always pushed for isolation and maintaining their traditional way of life while making frequent visits to the mainland to secure their sale of fresh produce. But Dahlia could see through this incongruity and never bought into it.

They proceeded to the poultry farm, which was only a short distance from Haven's End. An old tin shed specifically designed to house the hundreds of hens with space to roam. Provided with the best local grain for feed. No chemicals or antibiotics to supplement their diet—they were as natural as could be. The best eggs in the region came out of this farm.

"Oh, there he is, filling up the scrap bucket."

"We may need to get closer to the fence line so he can see us, Jack."

Surrounded by a steel picket fence with chicken wire, Paranormal Jack waved towards the Elder to get his attention. The feeding frenzy was on, and the hens were so loud that they drowned out the surrounding sounds.

"I think he's seen us," said Paranormal Jack. "And I don't think he's so happy we're here."

"I wouldn't worry too much, Jack. He's a grumpy old man at the best of times and not happy the police inspector is here." Dahlia crossed her arms and looked directly at the Elder, who was waiting to greet them at the picket fence holding two pails.

The Elder dropped his feeding pail on the ground only to be rushed by hens. In his knee-high gumboots, he walked through the soft ground towards them. Obviously dissatisfied, he rolled his eyes and bit his lips.

"And what brings you two here,' said the Elder while adjusting his farmer's swag hat with a string of corks dangling from it to keep away the flies.

"We want to go to Forsaken Rock and inspect the cave," said Dahlia.

The Elder dropped his smaller pail on the ground and stood upright, ready to burst into a lecture.

"Forsaken Rock, what did I hear you say?"

"Yes, and we know it's forbidden. That's why we're here." Dahlia's eyes glittered.

"You're serious, aren't you."

"Couldn't be more serious."

"You know you can't go there?" The Elder started to raise his tone.

"Yes, but you have never told us why," Dahlia responded sternly.

The Elder shook his head from side to side, refusing their request. "There is nothing for you other than misery and curse. And the less the town folk know about Forsaken Rock, the better."

"We know that's the reason Lady Jane was here with her assistant in the first place. We also know that's not the first time Mr. Gordon has visited the island. Do you know anything about that?"

Paranormal Jack interrupted. He had enough of being kept quiet and unleashed unusually.

"You must have endorsed their trip to Forsaken Rock. Someone must have guided them because it's hard to find. A cave perched on top of a cliff on the other side of the island and between a narrow passage."

The Elder remained quiet before responding to Jack's impromptu comment.

"Lady Jane contacted me through a distributor on the mainland. She was investigating the afterlife and wanted a guide to take them to Forsaken Rock. I warned her about the curse of Elijah Crane, but she wouldn't listen. She demanded I take her there.

"Hmm, how much did she offer you, Sir?" Dahlia was not holding back.

The Elder was red in the face as his blood pressure elevated. He rested by leaning onto the metal frame of the picket fence and sighed with a deep breath.

"Yes, she offered me money to take them there. But I needed it for my poultry farm. To expand production—new equipment and facilities for my hens."

"So, you compromised?"

"All the Elders engage in enterprise to make money. How do you think we support this town? Ever wondered why you have running water, all the food you can eat, and town facilities for all to share. Where do you think that money comes from? Surely, you're not that naïve."

Dahlia skilfully tried to dodge the question by focusing on the curse of Forsaken Rock.

"Tell me about the stone carved out by Elijah Crane. In fact, why don't you just come clean and describe what happened all those years ago? A colony settled on this island, and Elijah Crane was their leader. But something happened? He brought something with him—a curse—an evil pact?"

"The Elder didn't speak right away. He turned his

gaze toward the dark forest line, where the mist never seemed to lift, and the air tasted of rust and secrets. His crinkled face tightened, like leather left too long in the sun, as though an old wound had begun to throb.

"There was a colony," Paranormal Jack pressed. "They settled here—this island. Elijah Crane was their leader. But something happened. He brought something with him. A curse... an evil pact?"

The Elder exhaled, not in defeat, but as a man yielding to the truth.

"Yes," he said at last. "There was a colony, all right. A flock of believers following a man they thought was touched by the divine. Elijah Crane was a preacher... but he wasn't ordained by any god we'd recognize."

Paranormal Jack took a step closer.

"What did he do?"

"Elijah believed he could make a heaven on earth," The Elder said reluctantly while pointing to the sky. "But heaven isn't free, and it sure as hell don't come easy. He carved a stone black as pitch, smooth as a mirror, but it hummed. Vibrated like it had a heartbeat. He said it was a foundation stone, a gift from an angel who visited him in dreams."

Paranormal Jack's brow furrowed. "That wasn't an angel, was it?"

The Elder laughed once—a dry, humorless thing. "No. It was Betwixt, a demon." The name fell like a dropped hammer between them. The trees shuddered.

"Elijah built the religion on that stone," The Elder continued. "Used it as the cornerstone. Said it would keep them safe, bless the crops, and protect the children. And it did—at first. Crops grew taller, sickness vanished, even the tides obeyed him."

"But?"

"But the price came due." The Elder looked Paranormal Jack dead in the eyes. "Always does. The stone wasn't just a conduit. It was a prison. Or a door. Hard to tell. But Betwixt…that thing wanted out. And Elijah, fool that he was, thought he could strike a balance. Blood for blessings."

Paranormal Jack's stomach turned. "Sacrifices."

The Elder nodded. "Children went missing. Animals are twisted into things that shouldn't breathe. The whole colony slowly turned inward—paranoid, afraid. By the time the outside world came looking, the island was silent. Every one of 'em… gone. Swallowed by the very ground they tilled."

Paranormal Jack shivered. "And the stone?"

"They never found it," The Elder said. "But I've seen it. Deep inside the cave at Forsaken Rock. Still hums. Still waits. And if Elijah's writings were true… it's only dormant. Not dead."

"It's waiting to resurface to its previous glory?"

"Yes Jack, we contained it the best way we can. Put the stone away—out of prying eyes and visitors—tucked away deep in the cave all these years." The Elder paused and clutched onto his walking stick with both hands. "And I knew this day would come."

The sky was the color of old ash, stretching endlessly above them like a forgotten memory. It hung heavy, a veil of suffocating grey. Paranormal Jack, Dahlia, and the Elder made their way along the crumbling path that wound through the coastal woods. The ground beneath their boots was slick with moss, the air thick with the scent of damp earth and rotting leaves.

The Grave Wind followed them, persistent and restless, slipping through the trees like fingers searching for skin as if the land itself still mourned the secrets it held. It whispered, faint and cold, curling around Paranormal Jack's neck like a warning, the soft hiss of its passing filling the spaces between their footsteps. There was something hungry in it, something that gnawed at the edges of Paranormal Jack's consciousness, making the hairs on his arms stand at attention. But it maintained its distance, carefully watching from afar. It was gathering information and building a timeline.

Ahead, the Elder walked with his usual steady gait, his lantern swaying gently from his grip, casting long, skeletal shadows over the dense undergrowth. The light flickered like a heartbeat, illuminating the jagged edges of gnarled branches, tangled roots, and the occasional sharp stone that broke the surface of the earth. The lantern's glow kept the shadows at bay, but just barely. The woods were closing in around them, suffocating and alive, a place where the light was constantly struggling to push back against the dark.

Paranormal Jack and Dahlia trailed behind, his boots sinking slightly into the earth with each step, his mind more focused on the tin box than the path ahead. The box pressed against his chest; its weight familiar now—a part of him—but there was something else in the air. It felt heavier with each mile, as though the very ground knew where they were headed, as though the island itself was holding its breath, waiting for them to arrive. The air had a strange quality to it, like it was thicker than usual, as if the world around them was charged with an energy they couldn't place, something ancient and unnerving.

"You never said where Forsaken Rock actually is," Paranormal Jack muttered after a long silence, his voice cutting through the low murmur of the wind. He glanced at the Elder's back, squinting against the mist that clung to the trees. "It doesn't show up on any map."

The Elder's rough voice broke through the fog of Paranormal Jack's thoughts. "It's not meant to be on any map. Maps don't show things that were never meant to be found," he said with a gruff chuckle. "The island buries what it's ashamed of. Forsaken Rock is older than the lighthouse and older than the colony. Long before Elijah Crane brought his altar here, it was a place of offerings. Sacred. And cursed." His words carried weight, and Paranormal Jack could feel the pull of them settling deep in his gut. There was more to this place than anyone had let on.

Paranormal Jack's gaze flickered upward as they climbed higher, his boots finding purchase on the uneven ground. The trees thinned as they ascended, their twisted limbs and thick canopy receding. The air grew colder, sharper, as though the landscape itself had become more hostile the further they went. The once-welcoming woods now felt like a trap—tightly woven, with the sharp edges of the land clawing at them from all sides.

The land began to change beneath their feet—jagged stone pushing up through the dirt like broken teeth, sharp and unforgiving. The earth felt as though it was pushing back against them as if it didn't want them to continue. The wind had picked up, cutting through the trees with an urgency that made Paranormal Jack's chest tighten. Each gust carried the voices of the past, low and distant, like whispers from something beyond the veil, calling them forward or perhaps warning them away.

And then, the trees broke entirely, giving way to a stark, unrelenting view. The ground beneath their feet gave way to a sheer drop, the cliff edge falling away sharply to the endless grey sea below. The waves, cold and indifferent, crashed violently against the rock, sending salt spray into the air, mingling with the mist that hung like a shroud over the landscape. The world felt raw and exposed. Forsaken Rock. The name echoed in his mind as he stood at the edge, its weight pressing on his chest like the ocean itself was holding him there.

He turned to the Elder, but the older man had already begun moving forward, his lantern casting a small, steady light as he stepped carefully toward the altar. Paranormal Jack and Dahlia hesitated for a moment, feeling the gravity of the place settle in their bones. Something ancient lingered in the air—something that had never been fully understood, never entirely escaped.

The box tied around his chest seemed to pulse with the same eerie energy that hummed through the ground beneath his feet, its presence like a tether to this place—a connection to whatever had happened here, whatever darkness had been birthed on these rocks centuries ago. It was a beacon to Forsaken Rock.

The Elder reached the edge of the stone circle first, his lantern illuminating the weathered altar, now a fractured remnant of its once imposing grandeur. What had been built to honor and offer to the gods, or something darker, was now little more than a pile of crumbled stone, jagged edges jutting out like the bones of something long dead.

Paranormal Jack approached slowly, his heart pounding in his chest, the air thick with the presence of something that wasn't quite gone but not here either. He could feel the weight of the past pressing down on him. The altar was silent now, but it had once held power— Paranormal Jack could feel the remnants of that power in the air, like an aftertaste that lingered long after the meal had been eaten.

The Elder turned, his face half-obscured by the dim lantern light, his voice low but firm. "We're here," he said. "This is the place where the pact was made. Where it began and where it ends."

Paranormal Jack nodded, holding the tin box tighter, his fingers curling around it. The island had already taken so much from him, from them. But as they stood there in the shadow of Forsaken Rock, he felt something shifting. The air felt different now, heavier with purpose, and in the distance, he could see the faintest glimmer of light beginning to break through the clouds above the sea.

The wind whispered again, a soft moan at their backs, and Paranormal Jack knew they weren't alone.

There it was, Forsaken Rock. A flat, black slab jutted out over the sea like the tongue of a colossal beast. Storm-torn and slick with brine, the stone hummed underfoot—not with sound, but vibration. Paranormal Jack could feel it in his bones. A deep, slow pulse. Like something buried beneath it was dreaming.

"This is it," the Elder said grimly, stepping to the edge. "This is where Elijah Crane carved the altar stone. Where the colony gave their first blood. The altar was taken from this rock, which he had hewn by his hand and shaped with symbols, he said, came in visions."

They entered the main chamber of the cave, holding lanterns, barely exposing enough light against the dark walls. Suddenly, Paranormal Jack's scream echoed through the chamber as Elijah Crane's shape dissolved back into smoke, swallowed by the spiraling carvings in the cave walls. The plinth cracked down its center, releasing a deep, shuddering pulse that knocked Paranormal Jack and the Elder to the ground.

The stone in Paranormal Jack's arms—the tin box—rattled violently and then split open with a metallic shriek. A shard of obsidian shot out, hovering in the air, spinning like a compass needle gone mad. The carvings on the walls pulsed in answer, flaring with sickly green light.

Then came the voice. Not Crane's. Not Betwixt's.

It was Dahlia. Her scream wasn't from the world above. It came from *inside* the chamber, from *inside* the stone.

"Jack!" she cried, her voice thin and distorted, like it had been stretched across dimensions.

He scrambled to his feet. "Dahlia?"

Before he could speak again, the very air in the chamber warped—like the world exhaled. The stone walls rippled, and from the quartz veins, a mist spilled forth, curling like fingers.

At the edge of the chamber, a fissure opened on the floor. It wasn't wide, but it was *deep*—a narrow rift into nothingness, glowing faintly from within. Shapes flickered in the light. Faces. Screaming. Reaching.

Dahlia stood there. One moment, she was whole, standing on the ledge above the chasm, confused and terrified. The next, the mist surged and wrapped around her legs like vines. She tried to run—tried to call out—but the stone beneath her cracked and gave way.

Paranormal Jack lunged. "No!"

Too late.

She fell without sound, her body pulled into the rift. The glow flared—and was gone. The stone was sealed behind her like it had never opened. Silence.

Paranormal Jack hit the floor hard, hands outstretched, eyes wild. "Dahlia!" His voice echoed uselessly in the vast chamber.

The Elder knelt beside him, breathing hard, the lantern guttering in his grip. "The stone took her," he said, grim and quiet. "She's inside it now. Trapped in the *in-between*."

Paranormal Jack stared at the place where she had vanished, fists trembling. "Then we're not leaving. Not yet. I brought her back once. I'll do it again."

The Elder nodded slowly. "You'll have to go deeper. Beyond the plinth. Into what the island doesn't want to be remembered."

As if hearing him, the stone floor shuddered.

Another passage began to open—spiraling downward, lined with teeth-like rocks and whispering shadows. A path into the true heart of the curse.

Paranormal Jack picked up the tin box, which was now dark and still. He slung it over his shoulder and took a step toward the dark.

"Hold on, Dahlia. I'm coming."

And with that, they descended again—into a place where even the Grave Wind dared not follow.

9

THE FEEDING STONE

Paranormal Jack looked around. No trees. No birds. Even the sea below seemed to pull away from the cliffs, uneasy.

"What happened here?" he asked.

The Elder crouched near a dark scar in the stone—long like a blade had been dragged across it repeatedly.

"The final ritual. Elijah brought the children here. Betwixt demanded the purest soul to seal the pact. The parents followed blindly. By the time they realized what he'd become, it was too late. They tried to stop it—but the stone had already tasted blood."

Paranormal Jack looked away, bile rising in his throat.

The Elder stood and turned to face him.

"This is the stone's birthplace. And it's still tied to

the one beneath the keeper's cottage. If you want to reach Dahlia… truly reach her… you'll have to stand on this rock and open yourself to the spirit realm. It's a gate, Jack. But once you open it—there's no guarantee what comes through will let you leave."

Paranormal Jack stepped forward, the tin box warm in his hands. "I don't care. Dahlia's in there. I know it. I'll find her."

He knelt on the stone. Paranormal Jack began to light the incense—a strange, bitter mix of cedar and something older, something almost metallic. The Grave Wind surged, sudden and furious, whipping Paranormal Jack's coat as he opened the box.

The lock of Dahlia's hair shimmered faintly in the twilight. Paranormal Jack placed it on the stone and whispered her name.

"Dahlia…" The rock trembled.

From the cliff's edge, a shape began to form—not solid, not smoke. A liminal figure, blinking in and out of visibility, like a candle behind warped glass. Paranormal Jack leaned in. "Dahlia?"

Her voice came back cracked, layered, like multiple tones overlapping.

"Jack…you shouldn't have come here…," said Dahlia beyond the spiritual realm. Behind her, something stirred. Something vast. With too many eyes. And it was smiling.

Paranormal Jack shouted, but the wind swallowed his voice. His chest tightened. The Grave Wind curled around his ankles like smoke, whispering across the moss-covered stones with voices just below hearing. Dahlia. He could feel her presence in it now—faint, sorrowful, beckoning.

She's calling to me, he whispered.

The Elder stared at the rock like a man staring into a fire too long.

"Then it's time," he said finally. "If you're going to save her… if there's even a chance to rip her from Betwixt's grip, you have to go beneath."

"Into the cellar," Paranormal Jack said.

The Elder nodded. "Below the keeper's cottage. There's a trapdoor under the old rug by the hearth. No hinges. Just stone and salt to keep what lies beneath from coming up too easy."

"And the stone?"

"It's down there," The Elder said. "Elijah's altar. Covered in chains now—silver ones, laid by the last lighthouse keeper who knew the truth. Elias Gray. He hanged himself before Betwixt could finish him, but not before he tried to seal the place. That's why the

Grave Wind doesn't blow all the time. But now… it's slipping. The seal's breaking."

Paranormal Jack turned toward the keeper's cottage. It stood crooked in the mist, shutters banging gently in the windless air. It wasn't just a house anymore. It was a lid.

"You said the stone feeds," Paranormal Jack said. "So, if I go down there—"

"It'll know," the Elder finished. "Betwixt will feel you the moment you touch that trapdoor. It'll reach for you. Through memory. Through pain. Through her. Dahlia's spirit's been pressed against that veil for too long, Jack. She's not whole anymore. And what's left of her is tied to the stone."

Paranormal Jack clenched his fists.

"Then I need to untie her."

The Elder stepped forward and handed Paranormal Jack a small tin box wrapped in faded twine.

"Take this. Burn it down there. Incense, salt, a lock of hair you left behind. You'll need all three. It's the only way to call her spirit back from the threshold."

Paranormal Jack took the box and nodded.

"And one more thing," The Elder added. "You'll see things down there. Hear voices. They'll lie. They'll beg.

Some'll wear Dahlia's face. Betwixt is clever—it mimics what we love. Don't speak to it unless you're sure it's her."

Paranormal Jack turned back once more to the graveyard, where the wind moaned low through crooked headstones. Then he stepped toward the keeper's cottage, each footfall heavier than the last. The door creaked open on its own. Darkness waited inside. The moment the Grave Wind howled through Paranormal Jack's soul, reality fractured.

In one heartbeat, he could sense staring into Dahlia's flickering form. The next—he was falling. The sky peeled away like scorched parchment. The stone beneath him dissolved into black mist, plunging into darkness that wasn't empty but alive. He heard whispers — thousands, layered atop each other, speaking his name in tongues not meant for living mouths.

"Jack...you left her...come see what she's become," said Betwixt.

Then — stillness. Not silence, exactly. A place before sound. Paranormal Jack stood in a realm of greys and shadows, lit by an unseen source. Fog rolled at his feet. Strange, monolithic shapes loomed in the distance—ruins or broken altars. Above him, the sky churned like a black ocean hanging upside down. He was inside the threshold. Betwixt's domain.

"Dahlia!" he shouted, voice small in the endless quiet.

Footsteps echoed behind him. He turned—and there was Dahlia. Her hair was loose around her shoulders, eyes wet with tears.

"You came for me," she said, voice trembling.

Paranormal Jack took a step forward—then stopped. The Elder's warning rang like a bell in his mind: *Don't speak to it unless you're sure it's her.*

He narrowed his eyes and said, "What was the name of the beach where we found the message in the bottle?"

Dahlia blinked, confused. "What?"

Paranormal Jack stepped back. "You don't know."

Her face changed. Twisted. The skin seemed to melt, sag, and then stretch impossibly wide into a smile filled with far too many teeth.

"Clever," it hissed. "But not enough."

The thing lunged at Paranormal Jack, and with a flash of blue flame, it repelled the entity with a shriek of smoke and shadow. Then, the world shifted again.

He found himself standing in a hallway—one he recognized. The upstairs corridor of the keeper's cottage. Only now, it stretched on forever. Doors lined the walls. Behind each, he could hear muffled screams, sobs, laughter. He turned a knob at random.

Inside, a memory—his memory—played: he and Dahlia dancing in the kitchen, flour dust in the air, her laughter like sunlight. But something was off. The music playing was backward. Her eyes were hollow. And behind her, in the reflection of the kitchen window, something watched.

Betwixt was using himself against him now. He slammed the door shut. More laughter echoed through the corridor, now higher pitched, crueler. It came from the end of the hall, where a single door pulsed with dull red light. He approached, heartbeat thunderous. Inside that room, he knew, was Dahlia. Or what was left of her?

Paranormal Jack reached into his coat and pulled free the final item from the tin box—a small, tarnished mirror etched with protective runes. The Elder had called it the "truth glass." It would show what was real. He clutched it tight, stepped into the room—and gasped.

Dahlia was there, bound to the altar stone—the altar, its twin, embedded in this realm like a throne. Her body flickered, tethered by chains of mist and bone. Her eyes locked on Paranormal Jack.

It's really me, she whispered. *I'm still here.*

The room trembled. Something behind the altar began to rise—tall, shapeless, crowned with antlers and eyes that bled shadow. It was Betwixt.

It didn't roar. It didn't speak. It simply reached—

Paranormal Jack lifted the mirror. The image of Dahlia remained the same. No distortion. No lies.

It's her.

He rushed forward, heart burning, spirit shuddering. And the battle began. The altar pulsed beneath Dahlia like a beating heart carved from obsidian. Her eyes, though weary, locked on Paranormal Jack with fierce clarity.

"It's really you," she said again—but now there was no question.

Paranormal Jack nodded, stepping into the circle etched around the stone. The runes flared dimly under his boots, resisting his presence.

"I'm getting you out of here. We end this. now."

Betwixt towered behind her, a thing of shifting silhouettes and dripping starlight. Its face—or what passed for one—was a slow eclipse of eyes. Watching. Judging. Amused.

"You've brought light into the in-between," it

rasped, voice more thought than sound.

Paranormal Jack knelt beside Dahlia and placed the incense, salt, and mirror around its base in a triangle. He opened the final fold of the parchment the Elder had hidden in the tin box—a banishment rite older than the colony, older even than Crane.

"Can you move?" Paranormal Jack called out.

"I can try," Dahlia said through clenched teeth. The chains hissed as she strained against them.

Betwixt stepped forward—an impossible stride that folded space in on itself.

"You think words will undo what blood has built?"

"No," Paranormal Jack said, lighting the incense. "But the truth might."

The ritual began. Paranormal Jack spoke the invocation. Each word weighed more than the last, tugging at his bones. Smoke rose in curling tendrils—each one a memory. Her childhood laughter. Her tears. The last sunset they saw together. All fed into the smoke, building a bridge between her soul and the world she left behind.

Betwixt roared—not loud, but deep. The ground cracked and glowed with veins of red fire. The spirit chains tried to recoil, but Paranormal Jack pressed a hand to Dahlia's forehead.

"You're still you," he said. "Remember who you are."

Dahlia reached up with shaking fingers and touched the mirror. Her reflection blinked—and the chains faltered. The creature howled.

"Enough!"

Betwixt surged forward—but this time, Dahlia stood. Her feet hit the ground with force. The runes flared in response to her touch—accepting her. A burst of light erupted from the mirror, casting Betwixt into staggering contrast—too many limbs, mouths like wounds, wings made of broken prayers.

"I'm not yours," Dahlia said, voice hard and rising. "You fed on my fear. My grief. But I remember who I am."

She pulled the mirror and held it high.

"Jack," she said, "finish it!"

Paranormal Jack completed the final line of the incantation, slicing his palm and pressing it. Blood met salt. Reality bent inward.

With a scream that shook every corner of the realm, Betwixt fractured. Not slain—but driven back. Banished. Its body dissolved into spiraling threads of smoke and ash, sucked screaming into the dark folds between worlds. The floor cracked in two. The Grave

Wind surged one final time—then collapsed into silence. The grey fog lifted. The shadow realm faded.

Paranormal Jack and Dahlia collapsed together, gasping, clutching each other. The tin box lay scorched between them, its contents spent.

"You came back," Dahlia said.

"I never stopped trying,"

Far above, the lighthouse light finally turned.

10

ELIJAH CRANE

The cliffside loomed sharply and jagged above the crashing sea, winds howling like distant voices caught between the rocks.

The Elder knelt beside the fractured altar and brushed away centuries of moss and grit, exposing a faint spiral etched into the stone—concentric rings surrounding a jagged triangle that pointed straight toward the sea.

"Help me with this," The Elder muttered, already digging his fingers beneath a stone slab. Paranormal Jack joined him, and together they heaved. The slab groaned, then shifted with a grinding pop of disused hinges. A breath of cold, sour air surged upward like an exhale from something long buried. The stone fell away, revealing a narrow crevice hidden beneath the altar, too dark to be real. They stared into the opening.

The entrance was rough-hewn, barely wide enough for a man to fit through sideways. Its edges weren't worn smooth by time but jagged—as though clawed or carved in violent haste. Symbols ringed the mouth of the passage, etched deeply into the stone like warnings. They pulsed faintly in the lantern's glow, their edges glistening as if still fresh.

Paranormal Jack crouched at the threshold. "It's like the mountain bled to make this," he said quietly.

The Elder nodded grimly. "This wasn't a natural cave. This was cut open. Like a wound."

Inside, the walls were slick with condensation, the stone around the entrance damp and veined with dark mineral streaks that shimmered like oil. Long, twisting root systems hung down from above like fingers reaching for the living. The sound of the surf behind them faded, muffled by the oppressive stillness seeping from the cave.

They stepped inside. The air grew instantly colder. The Grave Wind, which had followed them like a whisper through the woods, refused to enter as though it feared what lay beneath. The lantern flickered once as if protesting, then steadied, its golden glow casting its elongated shadows far down the sloping tunnel.

A low, steady hum began—so faint it almost escaped notice—resonating through their boots and bones. It wasn't sound so much as pressure. A thrum beneath the skin. The heartbeat of the island.

Every surface inside the tunnel was marked with spirals, clawed glyphs, and long-forgotten language that defied understanding. Paranormal Jack brushed his fingers across one of the carvings—it was warm to the touch.

"The walls are alive," he murmured.

"No," said the Elder, voice low. "Something behind them is."

Farther in, the passage opened into a narrow stairway spiraling downward, carved from the bedrock with harsh, imprecise cuts. Water dripped from above in slow, steady plinks that echoed with unnatural sharpness.

As they descended, the entrance above shrank until it was just a slit of grey light, and then it disappeared entirely, swallowed by the dark. The cave had them now. And something inside it was waiting.

The stone staircase curved down in uneven spirals, each step slick with moss and something darker Paranormal Jack didn't dare name. Their boots echoed dully, but the sound didn't travel far—it was swallowed by the oppressive air, thick and unmoving. The further they went, the more the world above seemed like a dream receding into shadow.

The only light came from the Elders's lantern, its flame flickering against unseen drafts that brushed their cheeks but never stirred their clothes. The hum beneath their feet deepened—no longer faint, now a low, rhythmic pulse. Like breath. Or a waiting heartbeat.

The narrow stairway ended abruptly at a small landing, the ceiling low enough that they had to crouch. Ahead, the tunnel widened into a jagged archway of fused stone as if the rock had melted and then been pulled apart. The walls here bore deeper carvings—no longer just runes, but scenes.

Paranormal Jack held the lantern up. Figures writhed in the rock—twisted, elongated forms offering limbs to a towering thing with too many eyes and no face. Children are held above flames. A ring of hands encircling a spiral pit. At the center of it all, one name was scrawled repeatedly, its letters cracked and feverish: Crane. Crane. CRANE.

"Elijah," Paranormal Jack whispered.

The Elder didn't speak. His face was pale, tight around the eyes. He reached forward and placed a hand on Jack's shoulder.

"What we see from here on—don't trust it. This place feeds on memory. Guilt. It'll wear our own faces if it thinks it'll stop us."

They stepped through the arch. The chamber beyond was vast, hidden in the bones of the island. Its ceiling was vaulted like a cathedral, vanishing into darkness overhead. Veins of faintly glowing quartz lined the walls, casting a cold, unnatural luminescence. The light bent strangely in this place—shadows stretching in directions that didn't match the source.

And in the center of the chamber: the plinth. It stood crooked, cracked by time or by struggle. Chains wrapped around its base and vanished into the stone floor-like roots. Upon it lay the skeletal remains they'd glimpsed in the vision before—the bundle of blackened bones twisted into impossible shapes, fused with iron. Even now, they moved subtly, a slow shifting like breath. Like something dreaming in death.

Paranormal Jack approached slowly, each step dragging. The box in his hands had begun to vibrate. Whisper-thin voices spilled from its seams— muttering, pleading, laughing.

"It's awake," he said.

The Elder stepped beside him, lifting the lantern

high. As its light touched the plinth, the carvings on the surrounding walls flared. And something answered.

From the far side of the chamber, a shape emerged—slow and shuddering. A figure draped in shadow, its face hidden behind a veil of undulating black smoke. Eyes blinked open across its chest and arms. Mouths yawned where none should be.

Paranormal Jack stumbled back. The thing wore remnants of a robe, faded with age, crusted with salt. A crown of coral thorns sat upon its head, cracked and fused into the skull beneath. And around its neck hung a splintered medallion—half the symbol carved into the altar above.

"Elijah Crane." Called out the Elder. "Or what's left of him."

The figure did not speak. It simply raised one arm, and from the walls, the voices of the dead cried out— agonized, echoing, countless.

The curse was no longer sleeping. It had a voice. And Paranormal Jack knew they were now standing inside the oldest wound the island ever kept secret.

11

THE PASSAGE OF SPIRITS

T*he air on Forsaken Rock was still,* heavy with silence—not dread, but anticipation.

The altar lay in fragments, its symbols dimmed as if the very stone had exhaled a long-held breath. The last traces of Betwixt's essence had been banished, scattered like ashes into the folds of the in-between world. Yet something lingered—not malevolence, but souls. Lives frozen by Betwixt's widened fracture. The souls caught in the in-between had been freed to transition into the afterlife.

Paranormal Jack stood beside Dahlia, his gaze sweeping over the jagged remains of the altar. The rock beneath them hummed faintly, vibrating with the ancient memory of power once held there. The sky above the island shimmered—just faintly—as if gauze had been pulled away from the edge of vision, revealing a more profound clarity. And then, they appeared. One by one.

First came the lost colonists—gaunt figures in tattered, old-world garb. Their faces were shadowed by centuries of sorrow and struggle. Children clung to the sides of their parents, faces frozen in a quiet plea for release. Husbands reached for wives, their fingers trembling as they crossed the veil between life and death. One woman stepped forward, her hands clutching at her head in anguish, before slowly lowering them to reveal hollow eyes that for the first time in what felt like an eternity, began to fill with light. The light wasn't harsh or blinding, but soft healing.

Behind them came the keepers and sailors—figures bound to the island by fate and duty. Their coats, once vibrant, were now mottled with brine and age, and the lanterns they carried swayed gently on phantom hips, their light long extinguished. Some walked with limps, others dragging the wounds that had killed them in life. But none of them carried the weight they had before. The weary burden was gone—replaced by the calm of release, the final lifting of chains.

Among them, the broken, tortured soul of Elias Gray stepped forward. His eyes, once consumed by madness and despair, now held a gentle clarity. His neck, once bent under the weight of the noose of his own making, lifted with a grace that seemed almost foreign to him. The key that had once weighed so heavily around his neck now felt weightless. Elias looked up at Paranormal Jack, meeting his eyes with an expression of deep, silent gratitude.

With a trembling hand, he removed the key and placed it gently in Paranormal Jack's palm—a gesture of thanks.

Paranormal Jack's breath caught. It wasn't just the key to the lighthouse keeper. It was something more. Something that bridged the gap between the living and the dead. And then came Mr. Gordon, as he winked and nodded in gratitude by dipping his hat in a gesture of respect.

Then, the light came. A vertical shaft of pure, soft radiance—a shaft glowing like a moon on water—opened above the stone. It was not fire. Not wind. Just peace. A peace that filled the air, the stone, the broken ground. And as it bathed the spirits in its soft glow, they moved into it without fear. There were no cries.

No regrets. Just a quiet, collective sigh as they passed through the threshold into the unknown.

As the spirits ascended, the fog that had gripped the island for generations began to dissipate—slowly at first, like smoke curling upward. The mist lifted from the land as if it, too, had been waiting for this moment. The grass along the cliffs grew greener, the soil richer. The scent of rot that had haunted the shore vanished like a bad memory, replaced by the clean, salty air of a fresh morning. Even the Grave Wind—that relentless, tortured force that had once moaned and wailed through the hills—fell silent. Its voice is no longer twisted by torment. No longer bound to the island. It was finally still.

Dahlia stood beside Paranormal Jack; her eyes closed as the first tear slipped down her cheek. She had cried so much it seemed like all her tears had already been spent. But this was different. These were tears of release. She wept, not in sorrow, but in the quiet, solemn relief of knowing it was over.

It's over, she whispered, as though speaking to the winds, to the spirits, to the island itself.

Paranormal Jack said nothing, his gaze fixed on the horizon, where the shaft of light still pulsed above Forsaken Rock. The lighthouse, its stone now warm and alive, stood at attention. The cursed flame had long since been extinguished, but now it was free. No more flickering. No more whispering voices in the stone. Just light. Real, steady light.

Though Crinkled Face Joe's body was nowhere to be seen, his presence was undeniable—here, in the wind, in the quiet echo of the land, in the weight of the moment. Crinkled Face Joe had been with them all this time. And now, in this peaceful end, he was still with them.

The light above Forsaken Rock dimmed, folding in on itself like the closing of an eye, gentle and final. The gate had been shut, the rift sealed. And the island, finally, was free. The light closed behind them and, with it, the thin veil between worlds.

Paranormal Jack and Dahlia stood at the edge of Forsaken Rock, not speaking, just listening. Not for ghosts but for their absence. The absence of the pain, the torment, the voices that had long plagued them. And in that stillness, there was something they hadn't felt in what seemed like lifetimes.

Silence. Peace. It was a rare commodity on Solitary Island.

No more shadows crawling beneath the floorboards. No more voices behind the mirror. No more Grave

Wind moaning across the hills. No more restless spirits longing to return to the world of the living. Only the sound of wind through sea grass and the waves pulling gently at the shore. Like it used to be before the settlers arrived.

They walked back to the keeper's cottage slowly, their footsteps light, as if the very earth beneath them had shifted, giving them space to breathe. Each step felt as though the island itself was releasing them, letting them go. The air had changed. The sky was clear and crisp, unburdened by the weight of centuries of pain. Even the birds had returned—gulls, terns, the distant call of something winged and wild. It was a world alive again.

Dahlia reached for Paranormal Jack's hand and found it warm, steady. She looked up at him, and her voice was soft but sure.

"Do you feel it?" she asked, as though testing the truth of what she felt in her chest.

He nodded. His heart was light in a way he hadn't felt before.

"The weight's gone."

At the threshold of the keeper's cottage, Paranormal Jack paused and looked ahead. The lighthouse, a towering silhouette against the rising sun, stood tall and still—no longer a sentinel of sorrow but simply stone and glass and light. The light that no longer flickered with the curse of Betwixt but now shone steady and true.

Far beyond, Forsaken Rock lay at rest, its jagged edge softened by the mist like a wound finally healed.

12

THE LAST NIGHT

The winds that swept across the island were different now.

No longer the Grave Wind but a gentler, salt-laced breeze that rustled the grass and whistled soft through the shattered shutters of the keeper's cottage.

Paranormal Jack stood at the edge of the bluff, watching the sea. The sun had finally risen. It painted the sky in soft amber and blood-orange, bleeding warmth across the waves. Behind him, the lighthouse was silent. No more flicker of cursed flame. No more whispering stones. Just stone and light.

Inside the cottage, Dahlia blinked against the sunlight streaming through the broken window. Her eyes, still tired, were her own again.

He came in quietly with a cup of warm tea pressed into her hands.

"You slept," he said.

"I dreamed," she replied, her voice still scratchy, but something about it sounded like healing. "Not the bad kind."

Paranormal Jack nodded. He'd seen enough of bad dreams to last a lifetime. He sat across from her, watching her fingers wrap around the cup as if it were something fragile, something onto which she could hold.

They sat in silence for a while. The room was quiet—except for the soft creak of the keeper's cottage as it settled into the morning light, as if it, too, had finally exhaled. The air outside was filled with the sound of life returning gulls calling, the distant crash of waves against rocks, and the whisper of wind through the trees. A normal wind and not the sinister kind.

Paranormal Jack's gaze wandered out the broken window to the lighthouse, its towering silhouette now serene against the soft glow of the sky. He hadn't realized how much of himself had been tied to its cursed light, how much of the island's darkness had seeped into his own soul. But now, it stood in silence. No more shadow. No more pull. No more Betwixt to contend with.

He glanced at Dahlia, and for the first time in what felt like forever, he didn't see the fear in her eyes. Just quiet strength. It was as though the final veil had been lifted.

"Do you think it's really over?" Dahlia asked, at last, her voice tentative, still evaluating the weight of the question.

Paranormal Jack didn't answer right away. He looked around the room at the remnants of their battle—the scorched mirror and incense on the mantle, the dust and soot from the ritual still hanging in the air. "The stone's broken. The pact is gone. Betwixt is banished. That much I know."

"But?"

He turned toward the window, his eyes tracing the distant outline of Forsaken Rock, swallowed now by the morning mist. A place of memories. A place of broken things.

"Some things don't leave scars you can see. Doors, once opened, never close. We shut it as best we could."

Dahlia sipped the tea, her hands steady, the tremor of the past finally absent.

"I still feel him... sometimes. But it's different. Like he's fading."

Paranormal Jack's gaze softened. "The evil is gone. We made sure of that. It's just...lingering on the edge now. It won't reach for you again."

She closed her eyes and took a deep breath as if she were breathing in the peace of the island.

"I want to believe you."

He stood, walking to the window, his fingers grazing the sill where the wind had worn the wood smooth.

"You will. It's just going to take time. But you've got it now. Time and peace. We both do."

Dahlia set the cup down carefully, then reached across the table, taking his hand. Her fingers were warm, her grip solid.

"Crinkled Face Joe would've liked to see the sunrise," Paranormal Jack said quietly, his voice soft with the memory of their fallen mentor.

Dahlia nodded, her eyes glistening with the sting of unshed tears.

"He did. He saw it through us."

They sat like that for a long while, wrapped in silence and healing and something like peace. There were no more words left to say. Just the quiet hum of the island, the soft rhythm of their breathing, and the growing light of the morning sun.

The old clock on the wall ticked quietly, marking the passage of time—but for once, it didn't feel like it was racing.

When they finally packed the last of their things, Paranormal Jack slipped out of the cottage and took one last walk down to the shore. The island was different now. The air was clean and unburdened. The old, twisted trees on the cliffside appeared taller as if relieved from a heavy burden.

A small cairn of stones marked a grave no one had dug—just a place, really. A place where the island had finally exhaled the curse, where the wind blew clean for the first time in centuries.

He knelt and placed Crinkled Face Joe's old ribbon atop the stones, the same compass that had guided them all this time. A ribbon that had led them to answers and to sacrifice.

No more drifting, Paranormal Jack whispered, a final promise to his fallen friend. "Thank you."

The sun shone on the ribbon, gleaming like a final change of light in the quiet world they were leaving behind.

Back at the dock, the old boat rocked gently. Dahlia stepped aboard first, steady on her feet, and the sound of her boots lit the wood as though she were no longer carrying the weight of a thousand ghosts. Paranormal Jack followed, glancing once over his shoulder at the lighthouse, standing still, mute in the dawn. And then they left the island behind.

The boat sliced through the waves, and the island gradually faded from view. They rounded the headland, and the sun struck the broken lens of the lighthouse tower. For a fleeting second, the lantern flared once more, a final, brilliant flash of light across the sea—a final blink. Not cursed. Just light.

There was no hurry, no fear. The weight of the past was gone. There was nothing to escape, nothing to outrun. Only the sea ahead, calm and welcoming.

As the engine hummed to life, the boat rocked gently as if the island itself were saying goodbye. Dahlia sat at the bow, her face to the wind, her eyes closed, feeling the freedom in every gust that passed through her. Paranormal Jack stood beside her, one hand resting on the tiller, the other holding the rusted key that Elias Gray had given him. The key wasn't a burden anymore. It wasn't a token of suffering. It was a reminder. A reminder that even the cursed can be unbound. That even the lost can come home.

The sun rose higher, casting its golden rays across the water, as the island began to fall away into the mist behind them. The sea was calm. The wind was kind. They waved goodbye to the Elder in the distance, saddened by their departure—but he understood their predicament. There were more Solitary Islands to discover, as well as other lighthouses. Because the paranormal does not sleep or restrict itself to one location. Evil is everywhere, and it has its own calling card. They knew Dahlia and Paranormal Jack were coming,

The End

FROM THE AUTHOR

I hope you enjoyed reading Grave Wind as much as I loved writing it. If you had a positive experience, I would be grateful if you left an Amazon review by clicking the link below and leaving a few lines. Reviews help build my audience and readership and are an excellent product endorsement.

Regards,
Janice

https://www.amazon.com/dp/B0DJGQ6F9J

Join my author mailing list to receive updates free offers, and to connect with me.

All new subscribers receive a free copy of the series starter, The Girl in the Scarlet Chair.

https://preview.mailerlite.io/preview/487954/sites/91808440648729783/janicetremaynenewsletterlist

ABOUT THE AUTHOR

Janice Tremayne is an Australian author who lives with her family in Melbourne. Her Haunting Clarisse Series reached number one on the Amazon Kindle ranking for Occult, Supernatural, and Ghosts and Haunted Houses categories for hot new releases and bestsellers.

Janice is a finalist in the Readers' Favorite 2020 International Book Awards in fiction-supernatural and was awarded the distinguished favorite prize for paranormal horror at the New York City Big Book Awards 2020. She recently received a silver medal at the 2021 IPPY Book Awards for Australia/New Zealand/Pacific Rim—Best Regional Fiction. In 2023, she received the Titan Gold Book Award for excellence in writing.

Janice is well-versed in her cultural superstitions and how they influence daily life and customs. She has developed a passion and style for writing ghost and supernatural novels for new adult readers.

Her books contain heart-thumping, bone-chilling, thought-provoking ghosts and paranormal experiences that deliver a new twist to every tale.

THE HAUNTING CLARISSE SERIES

She never signed up to be a spirit hunter. Hunting down demons? But evil spoke to Clarisse and changed her life forever.

Enjoy over one thousand pages of intense, nail-biting, and spinetingling demonic encounters in real Australian ghost towns.

Clarisse never imagined her first encounter with demons would be in her home. A scarlet chair with a two-hundred-year-old curse bound by superstition. Hell-bent on destroying relationships, this evil presence wants her out of the way.

She meets her soul mate and joins him, visiting remote ghost towns. But supernatural battles lay waiting as local demons summoned her. Can she convince her skeptical partner that it takes more than intuition to rid these towns of entrenched evil?

Can Clarisse withstand the sharp-talking demons that latch onto her with sinister motives? Will she cleanse the ghost towns from their curse?

These evil encounters become an affliction of the mind. A risk to herself and her partner that could result in death.

Suppose you like a fast-moving, heartfelt, and nail-biting supernatural horror guaranteed to raise your heartbeat. In that case, you'll love this series by the 2020 USA Readers' Favorite International Book Awards Finalist in Supernatural Fiction, Janice Tremayne.

Pick up your copy today and join the battle for good versus evil.

Book One: The Girl in the Scarlet Chair
Book Two: Haunting in Hartley
Book Three: Haunting in Old Tailem
Book Four: The Infant Spirits
Book Five: The Charterhouse of Evil
Book Six: The Nowhere Room

https://www.amazon.com/gp/product/B089GXH9JV

Grave Wind